When the Stars Lead Home

LAURA WEIGEL DOUGLAS

ISBN 978-1-63575-466-7 (Paperback)
ISBN 978-1-63575-467-4 (Digital)

Christian Faith Publishing, Inc.
296 Chestnut Street
Meadville, PA 16335
www.christianfaithpublishing.com

Printed in the United States of America

Dedication

To Isla, you are my joy, my purpose, my blessing. I hope you have many adventures in life and know that when the stars lead you home, I will always be there.

Chapter 1

Plan A had been to lead a normal life. I can scratch that one off my list, Tizzy thought. Plan B would have been to at least stay here at home with Ruthie watching over her, but Ruthie said sixty-eight is too old to be watching over a twelve-year-old girl, and besides, her parents had written it differently in their will. Tizzy mentally ticked Plan B off her list of options. What was about to happen to her now, she realized, could not even be called Plan C. *This was more like Plan K, maybe even Plan O,* she thought then frowned, a crease deepening between her eyebrows.

"Tizzy? Tizzy? Are you listening to me?"

"Hmmm? Oh, yeah, sorry. Eleven o'clock?" Tizzy looked up at Ruthie apologetically.

"They're coming on the eleven-o'clock flight, which means they should be here by two." Ruthie, the camp cook who had lived here all of Tizzy's life, looked down at the girl with concern. She wasn't so sure about how this was going to work out either.

"I probably won't be here," Tizzy's gaze wandered out the kitchen window, "I've got chores to do."

"Like what? No chore is more important than welcoming your aunts."

Tizzy wracked her brain. "The horses need feeding, and I have to muck the stalls." Tizzy's voice slowly faded out as she tried desperately to come up with more things she could list in order to avoid the arrival of the two aunts she had only met twice, and that had been years ago.

"Greeting them when they come in would be the right thing to do, Tizzy. They lost a sister too." Ruthie tried to put her arm around Tizzy but she pulled out of reach.

"Losing a sister isn't the same thing as losing both your parents." The frustration and sadness in Tizzy's voice came to its peak. Tizzy turned away from Ruthie and slumped against the wood countertop in the kitchen. "They hardly knew my mom, and they don't know me at all," Tizzy retorted.

Ruthie took in a deep breath and looked at the young girl she loved like a granddaughter. She knew what she was about to say would surprise her. "That's not quite the truth, honey. Twenty years ago when this camp was still in its heyday, those three girls, your mom and aunts, ran around here like they were some wild tribe of adventurers. They grew up here on this island and were not only sisters but best friends. Sometimes life takes people in different directions, but it can't erase the past. The bond those girls shared is still there." Tizzy raised an eyebrow at Ruthie, doubtful that her mom could ever have been so close to two aunts she had rarely heard from and barely seen. "Listen, Tizzy." Ruthie rested her arm on Tizzy's shoulder and gave her a slight squeeze. "We have the rest of this summer, okay? Who knows what the future holds for the camp or for us. Let's give this summer our best shot." Ruthie gave Tizzy a wink out of her old light-blue eyes and turned back to the dough she was making for the welcome home pie.

"What if I don't want them to stay?" Tizzy moaned and slumped even further against the counter.

"Do you want the camp to remain open so you can keep living here?" Ruthie asked.

"Yeah."

"Then you don't have a choice."

*****

The cab smelled of sweaty armpits and dirty feet. The odor was amplified by the quiet in the taxi as the two sisters sat in silence. Cole, an artist with jet-black hair and tan skin, stared out the window at the Douglas fir trees that edged the side of the road. Every once in a while, through a gap in the greenery, she spotted the Puget Sound, just a few yards away but mostly blocked from view by the forest. *Just like life,* she thought, *sometimes you can't see the huge and endless possibilities that lie directly in front of you.*

Cole turned to Lindsay and looked at the sister she had not seen for the last four years. They talked on the phone now and again, but Lindsay was so busy with work that she always seemed distracted. They hardly ever had a chance to really catch up. "When was the last time you saw Tizzy?" Cole asked.

Lindsay popped her head up, her blonde pony-tail bouncing off the seat, and opened her eyes. She had been trying to sleep on the cab ride from the ferry, if only to help block out the stink in the car. "Maybe five years ago? Let's see, she's twelve now. I think Ann and Jack brought her out to New York when she was seven. They had some sort of camp owner's conference they were attending in Jersey. They stopped in for a few days to visit. Cole," worry entered her voice, "she was just a baby then." Lindsay rested her hands on the leather briefcase that sat on her lap and drummed her fingers. It was a nervous habit she had, the only thing that gave away her true feelings. Otherwise, Lindsay was the picture of confidence—*she always has been*—Cole thought to herself.

"I haven't seen her since about that same time." Cole confessed. Cole lived in Nevada, in the desert where she made pottery that sold at local galleries. "That was back when the camp was still doing relatively well and Ann and Jack felt like they could afford to travel. Tizzy probably won't even recognize us."

Lindsay crossed her ankles, smoothing out the pant leg of her expensive designer suit. "Listen, Cole, we're just here for the summer. That was the agreement, then it's back to normal life. I feel horrible about what happened to Ann and Jack. The car accident was only two months ago and Tizzy has barely had time to wrap her head around it, but this is the best we can do."

"Thank God Ruthie has been able to take care of her and the camp. Ruthie always took care of everything," Cole interjected. She could see that Lindsay was beginning to tear up.

Lindsay shook her head to clear away the sadness and quickly got back to reality. "I only have two and a half months off work, then I have to be back, or I for sure won't get the promotion I've been expecting. We owe it to Ann to take care of Tizzy, but we can't leave our lives to care for a summer camp too. We're only going through with this last summer because the kids are already signed up and paid for. It'll also help Tizzy adjust to life without her parents…and with us." Lindsay fixed her eyes on Cole, making sure her sister was listening. "Then in the fall, we'll sell the camp, and Tizzy can go to the Evergreen School for Girls. I found a boarding school that was located right in between you in Nevada and me in New York so we can each visit a few times a year. I know it's not ideal, but it's our only option. Neither one of us is set up to be a mom, let alone run a summer camp," Lindsay finished with a huff.

Always the voice of practicality and reason, Cole thought. Although deep down, Cole knew Lindsay was right. She wasn't ready to take on a summer camp or a child. She loved her memories of Green Hills Adventure Camp and all the fun she had growing up there after her parents bought the land and built the cabins. It had been quite the adventure for the family to start its own business, let alone invite groups of kids every couple of weeks throughout the summer to live with them on their property. Cole couldn't deny that she had been given an amazing childhood, but who knew what the camp was like now? Ann had written earlier this year telling both sisters that they were having a hard time keeping up with all the costs. Parents just weren't sending their kids to adventure camps anymore, especially not with the opening of two new camps on the island. The European Riding Academy for Girls and Still Waters, a sailing camp for privileged boys, had both put a huge dent in the income for Green Hills. Ann had written her sisters hoping they had some money they would like to invest in the camp. They needed new canoes and repairs for a few of the mountain bikes in order to stay competitive with the fancy new neighboring camps. Cole had given what little she could afford, and Lindsay had given much more; however, neither amount would have lasted long with the great expense of running a summer camp.

"Remember," Lindsay broke into Cole's thoughts, "it's just for the summer." The two sisters looked at each other, sadness in both their eyes at the thought of having to eventually break the news to Tizzy. They quickly turned to face forward and gasped. It had been so long, they both thought, as they passed under the carved wooden sign that announced they had arrived at Green Hills Adventure Camp.

Chapter 2

"Come on, Pip." Tizzy called to her dog to keep up with her. Pip was a medium-sized border collie/sheltie mix with black markings around her eyes so that it looked like she was wearing a bandit's face mask. She was Tizzy's best and one of her only friends. Tizzy and Pip made their way along an overgrown path that led toward the large white barn that housed most of the outdoor equipment. Tizzy made a mental note that the shrubs and weeds on the path would need to be cut back before the campers arrived next week. It was one of the many items on her father's list of things to do that had never been done. Now, Tizzy realized, they never would be, unless she did them. She highly doubted that either of her two aunts, one a big-time marketing business manager and the other an artist from the desert, would be up to hacking away at overgrown paths. "They probably won't be good for much of anything," Tizzy muttered under her breath to Pip, "except for bossing me around." That was the problem. She knew that in order for her to stay at Green Hills, she needed her aunts. That drove Tizzy crazy. Tizzy was fiercely independent and always had been. Carefully making her way amongst the rocky path, Tizzy remembered back to one of her favorite stories growing up. She used to beg her mom and dad to tell her stories about herself when she was younger. They would all curl up in her bed beneath the quilt her mom had sewn for her, and her parents would take turns telling Tizzy the story of how she got her name.

"You were born Tessa Mae McConnell. It was a name we had decided to pass on to you from my own grandmother who was born and raised here on Orcas Island," her mom would always start by saying.

Then Dad would take over, "It was clear from the very beginning that you were a strong, brave girl. You were never afraid to try things by yourself. You walked early, you were always climbing rocks down on the beach, you even rode that dapple gray horse we had before you could walk." Tizzy's dad would beam with pride.

"If Dad or I ever tried to hold you back or help you, you would throw a real hissy fit. You screamed and hollered and would lay on the floor and kick your little feet until we gave in and let you keep on doing whatever it was you decided you wanted to do.

We used to say to each other, 'Watch out, or Tessa Mae will throw a tizzy fit.' Somewhere along the line, we just started calling you Tizzy."

Tizzy's dad was always quick to jump in here and remind her, "Tizzy, your name means that you are strong and capable and adventurous. It means you're independent." He would smile teasingly at her, "Not just capable of throwing a fit. Although you did plenty of that too." Then he would laugh and tickle her and her mom until they cried, and when they finally all quieted down, they would lay there in her bed until she fell asleep. She would dream happy dreams about climbing mountains and kayaking across the Puget Sound and riding her horse through deep fields of grass, unafraid of anything, because she was Tizzy the Adventurer.

Tizzy looked up and realized she had already made it to the barn. She stopped just outside the door and reached down to pet Pip who was leaning heavily against her leg. "I'm okay, Pip. I just realized something." Pip looked up at her and tilted her head as if asking what it was that Tizzy now knew. "We have to keep the camp open. This is my home. This is all that's left of my mom and dad." Tizzy scrunched her eyebrows and frowned. "The only problem is, we need Cole and Lindsay in order to do it."

*****

"Hooolllyyy smokes," Lindsay let the words hang awkwardly in the air. "It doesn't look a thing like it used to, except the view." She pulled a pair of sunglasses from her handbag and slid them on as she stared out over the waters of the Puget Sound. Green Hills Adventure Camp was situated high up on a cliff on Orcas Island. The main building faced the blue-gray waters with such a spectacular view it took your breath away. Just below them, a path wound its way down the steep cliff face to the boat dock where a variety of kayaks and canoes were tied up.

"Well, we knew they were having financial problems," Cole said softly. "It doesn't look so bad. Nothing a new coat of paint and a lawnmower couldn't fix right up." Lindsay noticed that Cole's smile seemed forced, as if she didn't even believe herself.

The girls turned around to take in the whole scene. After entering through the main gate, they wound up the gravel road and ended up here at the clubhouse. This is where the campers ate meals and held the talent shows and skits they ended each session with. Just at the other end of an open field, now waist high in weeds and wild flowers, stood the cabins, eight of them all together—small wood structures with just the bare necessities, including an outhouse not far off.

"My girls, it's good to have you home." Lindsay and Cole turned at the same time to see Ruthie standing behind them, her arms wide open. Her smile was the exact same one they had grown up with, warm and loving. She had been much more than the camp cook to the three sisters. She had been a second mother. It didn't surprise Cole or Lindsay to see that Ann and Jack had kept her on after taking over running Green Hills. Ruthie seemed to belong here as much as the camp itself.

Cole and Lindsay both ran to Ruthie and leaned into her arms. They felt like they were twelve years old again, needing someone to hold their hands through this rough patch in life.

"Sorry it took us so long to come," Cole quickly answered. "We know the accident was a couple of months ago. It just took a while to figure out the extended leave for both of us so we could be here all summer."

"Don't you worry about it, honey." Ruthie's smile was forgiving. "You're here now. That's all that matters. Tizzy needs you both. You've got your work cut out for you."

"We can see that," Lindsay said and spread her arms out to take in the different areas of camp that had obviously gone uncared for in the last few months.

"It's been hard to handle everything around here as you can see," Ruth confessed, "but harder yet to care for a girl that lost both her parents." She could see sadness flash across the eyes of the two sisters. "The poor girl seems to be managing okay, but I think it's just because she has the camp to distract her. She's acting like she's going to do it all herself, run the camp, take care of the animals. She doesn't even know yet how much she needs you two."

"Well, we're up for the challenge." Cole grasped Ruthie's hand gently.

"At least for the summer," Lindsay reminded them, "that's all we can promise."

"Here she comes now." Ruthie looked off into the distance. All they could see was a growing cloud of dust. "That's her on Sprint. He's one heck of a barrel racing horse, sure lives up to his name. Tizzy and he have won all sorts of ribbons. She pretty much lives up there on his back."

As the cloud of dust grew closer, both Cole and Lindsay held their breath. They weren't sure how Tizzy would react to them staying on at the camp this summer. Ruthie had made it perfectly clear to them in letters they had been sending back and forth since the accident that Tizzy was trying to deal with this situation all on her own. They knew Tizzy felt they were interfering. What Tizzy didn't know was that if Cole and Lindsay didn't come stay the summer, she would have had to leave the camp to come stay with one of them. Neither of them were set up for that, so they didn't really have any other choice. Whether or not Tizzy realized it, this was her best option.

Ruthie walked out into the path that Tizzy and Sprint were racing in on. The brown-and-white paint horse didn't seem to be slowing down, and Lindsay was afraid she was going to have to jump into the road to push Ruthie out of the way, which she was sure would ruin her brand-new shoes. At the last minute, Tizzy reigned in Sprint hard. They came to a skidding stop, the horse almost sitting on its haunches. Ruthie didn't blink an eye.

"Get down here, young lady, and say hello to your aunts. They just got in." Ruthie's voice was stern but loving, just the way she had always been. She might have the title of camp cook, but the girls knew that she really ran the camp. Everyone listened to her, or they bore the consequences, which normally meant cleaning the outhouse.

Tizzy swung her legs out of the stirrups and hopped down. Sprint wore a Western saddle with a colorful blanket underneath. The saddle leather had "All-around Barrel Horse, San Juan County Rodeo, Tizzy McConnell 2015" engraved on its side.

"Hi," Tizzy mumbled and looked down at her brown leather cowboy boots.

"Hey, Tizzy, long time no see." Cole walked straight at her and gave her a big hug. Tizzy only flinched a little.

This is awkward, Tizzy thought, right before her other aunt came straight at her. The three of them stood in a cloud of dust hugging for what seemed like forever in Tizzy's mind. She had quickly noticed that her aunt Cole looked the part of the artist—long flowy skirt, lots of beaded necklaces, and her long dark hair had a slight wave to it. In contrast, Lindsay wore a business suit and high heels.

Pip saved them all from the nonstop hugging by barking and dancing around the three of them, nipping at their heels.

"Ouch," Lindsay said and hopped away, shooing the dog with her hands frantically, "she's biting me."

"Pip, come here." The dog immediately came to Tizzy's side and sat between her and the horse. "She's not *biting* you. She's a herding dog. It's her instinct."

There was a long pause when no one knew what to say. Tizzy held Sprint's reins and stroked Pip on the head. "Well," Ruthie came to the rescue, "why don't we let your aunts get settled in at the big house. I've cleared out their old rooms. Then we can all sit down for dinner and get to know each other."

"Sounds like a plan," Cole agreed.

Tizzy mounted Sprint in one fluid movement and looked down at her aunts. "I'm really glad you're here." Her voice was quiet and unsure.

"We're glad to be here, Tizzy," Lindsay answered back.

Tizzy looked first at her aunts and then finally at Ruthie. Her one ally stood between Cole and Lindsay, accepting them back as if they had never left. Tizzy sighed and gave a slight nudge to Sprint, and they were off at a gallop. Lindsay stepped back so fast she almost lost her balance, and Ruthie had to grab her arm to keep her upright. The three of them stared after Tizzy, her long dark braid flying behind her as if she couldn't get out of there fast enough.

*****

Back at the barn, as she untacked Sprint, Tizzy replayed her meeting with her aunts in her mind.

The funny thing was, what Tizzy had said was the truth. She *was* glad that her aunts had come. Not because she was so excited to see them but because she had realized that having them here was her only chance at keeping the camp. Although she had only met them a couple of times, they had always been nice to her. They sent her gifts for her birthday and for Christmas, and her mom had told her countless stories of the three of them growing up on this land. Her dad used to tease her mom and describe them as the original band of wild children on the island. *Distance doesn't change the past,* Tizzy reminded herself of Ruthie's words. Even though they had left and moved across the country, a part of them still belonged here, and somewhere in Tizzy's heart, she knew that. Now she just had to get the two of them to realize that. At least enough to see they didn't want to leave when summer ended. Tizzy now knew that if her aunts left, she would have to also. That was the last thing she wanted.

Chapter 3

The last week before camp began flew by. The ladies of Green Hills settled into an easy friendship of sorts. Even if it didn't seem like family yet, Tizzy thought, there was at least some hope. She liked her aunts for all their faults, and they had a few. Cole was a little spacey at times. She would start one project and then get sidetracked. She had begun cutting away at the open field with the riding lawn mower and left the job half done when she spotted a beehive on the corner of the shed and ran off to get her drawing pad and pencils. She had spent hours sketching the hive while she should have been working. Tizzy came in behind her and finished up the mowing.

Lindsay, on the other hand, had made list upon list of things that needed to be done to make the place presentable. Actually doing the chores, however, wasn't Lindsay's cup of tea. She complained about getting dirty, tired easily, and seemed better suited to be the boss. Yet somehow, with Ruthie's help, they managed to get Lindsay's endless list of chores completed just in time for the campers to arrive on Monday.

*****

Sunday night, Tizzy called her best friend Ashton, "You wouldn't believe it, Ashton, they're nothing like her. My mom was like the ultimate cowgirl, and they're," Tizzy paused, trying to think of the best way to describe her two aunts, "not."

"Well, they can't be all bad." Ashton, always the voice of reason, chimed in.

"They're not, I guess. They're both actually pretty funny in a way. Lindsay is a total business lady. She's literally the definition of a city slicker. She's always wearing these fancy outfits and has her hair and makeup all done up every single day. I can tell she's really smart, though. She's on her way to being a partner in some marketing firm in New York City. Cole, on the other hand, is the total opposite. She's kind of hippie-ish. I see her out on the bluff every morning doing yoga. She's really nice, though. I guess she kind of reminds me of my mom. She's always checking on me and trying to get me to do things with her."

"That doesn't sound too bad." Ashton said.

"I guess not. I wish you could've stayed on the island this summer. Things would've been so much better if you could've been at camp with me."

"Tell me about it! Trust me, I wasn't the one who wanted to go off to Quebec for a whole summer. They don't even speak English here!" Jake, Ashton's twin brother, had convinced their parents that it would be a "cultural experience" for the family to live in another country for the summer. Ashton's parents had signed up online for a house swap with an elderly couple from Quebec.

"Well, I hope you have a good time. I'll be busy here anyways. I've got eight weeks to convince my aunts that one of them needs to move here or at least let me stay here with Ruthie after the summer ends."

"You'll do it, Tizzy, you don't belong anywhere else."

Tizzy and Ashton hung up, and Tizzy sat up on her bed. She looked around her room at all her barrel-racing ribbons and the pictures of her with her parents hiking in the Olympic National Forest. She had framed photos of them mountain biking in the woods behind the camp and rock climbing off of Highway 2. Her dad had always been stopping to take pictures of them, which at the time had seemed annoying, but now she was glad that he had. Tizzy picked up a picture of her mom, dad, and her summiting Mt. St. Helens from last spring. "How am I going to do it? How am I going to remind Cole and Lindsay how much they love it here? I'm exhausted already." Tizzy lay down with the picture of her parents beside her and fell asleep, knowing that in less than twelve hours, thirty new campers would be arriving at Green Hills.

Chapter 4

Ruthie lined up all the campers on the freshly mown field facing her, Cole, and Lindsay. "Here at Green Hills Adventure Camp, we focus on the three *B*s: biking, boating, and barrel racing. We don't think it makes any sense to let the boys have all the fun with the adventure sports, right?" The campers all cheered. "We have mountain biking trails in the woods behind the main building, kayaks and canoes down on the dock, and a large horse barn that is set up with an awesome herd of barrel racing horses." Tizzy had heard this opening speech a thousand times. Ruthie was reciting it perfectly, just as her mom and dad had at the beginning of every camp session.

This group of campers were the youngest they would have all summer. They were mostly third and fourth graders from the Seattle area. She wondered how many of them had ever ridden a horse before, let alone a barrel racing horse. Well, that's what she was there for. She loved the Green Hills horses and was always on hand at the barn making sure everything went smoothly.

"Now, girls," Ruthie continued, "while you're here, you need to stay on camp property. Our camp is bordered by two others, Camp Still Waters to the south, which is a sailing camp for boys, and the European Riding Academy, which is an all-girls English equestrian camp to the north." This part of the speech was new, Tizzy realized, as this was the first year for the boys camp on the island and only the second year for the girls English riding camp. The European Riding Academy had done well last year, Tizzy remembered overhearing her parents say it had cut into their business. At least they didn't have to worry about the boys' camp taking away any customers since Green Hills was an all-girls camp.

Ruthie finished her speech, including the rest of the camp rules, and then the campers broke up into eight cabin groups and went off with their counselors, girls from the local high school who worked here every summer. Lindsay and Cole looked at each other with relief as the kids ran off. They both knew how lucky they were to have these experienced camp counselors on hand. The last thing they needed was to have thirty eight-year-olds under their wing without any help.

*****

Later that night, Cole went into town to the island's general store. Miller's Hardware and General Store had been on the island as long as Cole could remember. She found parking right out front and got out of the old Chevy truck that Ann and Jack had owned for years. Walking into Miller's, Cole was reminded of growing up on this island, all the times she rode her bike to this very store with her two sisters to buy an ice cream cone, always chocolate chip mint for her. It was amazing how much time had passed and how different things were. She was so lost in her thoughts that she ran straight into the back of someone as she entered the store.

"Oh, I'm sorry!" Cole apologized, embarrassed.

The man she had ran into turned around and smiled. "No problem, don't worry about it." He was about her age, with dark hair and a beard. He had dark skin and brown eyes that crinkled at the edges. "I'm Danny. You must be new to town."

"I'm Cole. It's nice to meet you, and actually, I'm just back in town for the summer. I grew up here."

"Really? That must have been awesome. I grew up in Montana but used to visit here once or twice a summer, just when my family was dropping my sister off or picking her up from camp."

"What camp?" Cole asked.

"It's called Green Hills Adventure Camp. My sister went every year for six years straight, couldn't get enough of the place. I was always jealous that they didn't take boys."

Cole laughed. "What are the odds? I grew up there. My parents owned the camp, I probably knew your sister. My youngest sister, Ann, took over the camp when my parents retired, and my other sister and I are back in town for the summer to help transition things with my niece, Tizzy. Ann, Tizzy's mom, just passed away a few months ago."

"I'm so sorry, I heard about that. I actually run the Still Waters sailing camp, so I'm your neighbor. I met Ann and Jack just a couple of times over the last year while we were setting up. Seemed like really nice people."

"They were," Cole replied. "Anyways, it was really nice to meet you. I'm sure I'll see you around, Danny."

Danny smiled at Cole and shook her hand. This was going to be a hard summer for her, he thought, as he left the store and turned to look back at her.

*****

Tizzy woke up early every morning to go for a ride on Sprint. It was a habit she had picked up from her dad. He liked to ride the camp grounds before anyone else was even up. Sometimes she would join him. He would always tell her stories from when he was growing up in Wyoming as they rode along the fence line. That was what he loved most about Green Hills, he would always say, it gave his daughter and other girls a chance to have the same adventures he had growing up. Those early-morning rides were some of the best times Tizzy had with her dad. She learned a lot from him and now felt closest to him when she was out riding the camp grounds as the sun rose.

"Whoa, Sprint. Hang on a minute." Tizzy pulled up next to a break in the fence line that bordered the northern edge of the property. It looked like the wire had been loosened or pulled aside. Tizzy dismounted and landed softly on the mossy ground. "That's weird," she said to herself. She made a mental note to have Ruthie tell the handyman who came out once a week to have it repaired. Tizzy walked back to her horse and grabbed a handful of Sprint's dark-brown mane before swinging her leg up on his back. She always preferred to ride bareback in the early mornings, just like her dad.

*****

Lindsay was on her cell phone at the kitchen table, holding a mug of coffee, when Tizzy walked in the front door. Tizzy could hear her talking to her boyfriend Chandler, something she did every morning while he rode the New York subway into work on Wall Street. He was a stock broker—something that Lindsay was very proud of. "I *realize* that, Chandler," she sounded annoyed. "I don't know how Jack and Ann kept the camp afloat this long." She paused to listen to Chandler's response, and Tizzy stopped. She didn't want Lindsay to know she was listening. Standing in the entryway, Tizzy stayed out of sight. "I'm going to send you a spreadsheet with the cost of repairs and upkeep, the cost of keeping the animals, and the mortgage and land taxes. Compare it with the income list I sent you. I just don't know if it's even possible at this rate to keep the place open. It'll break Tizzy's heart, Ruthie's too, but I don't know if we'll even have a choice come fall." Tizzy turned around and opened the door and then slammed it shut so that Lindsay would know that she was back. She took off her boots and barn jacket and left them in the entryway.

"Morning," Tizzy said with all the cheer she could muster.

"Good morning, sunshine." Lindsay smiled up at Tizzy as she came in and sat down next to her. In the last few weeks, Lindsay's style had relaxed, Tizzy noticed. She now wore a flannel shirt over skinny jeans and tall black leather boots. She still wore several gold bracelets and looked beautiful with a loose ponytail, but she definitely looked more like she fit in on the island.

"Who were you talking with? Chandler?"

"Yeah, just about some business stuff of his. Kind of boring actually." Tizzy felt bad acting like she hadn't heard Lindsay's conversation, but Lindsay wasn't being honest either, so Tizzy figured they were even. What worried her was that Lindsay felt the camp's financial future was concerning enough to talk to Chandler the stock broker about it.

"Did you have a good ride this morning?" Lindsay asked, changing the subject.

"Yeah, it's already warming up." Early July in Washington wasn't usually this warm, but they were having a great summer so far, ideal for campers. "I did see something kind of weird, though. There was a break in the wire fence on the north side of the camp. Almost like someone had pulled it apart."

"That's odd." Lindsay tilted her head.

"Yeah, I'll tell Ruthie when she comes up and ask her to call the handyman." Ruthie lived in her own little cottage on the west side of the property. "I just can't figure out how it happened, though."

"Some sort of animal probably," Lindsay guessed.

"Maybe," Tizzy said, but she didn't think so.

Just then, Cole walked in wearing her yoga pants and a blue printed scarf. She leaned down and gave Tizzy a kiss on the cheek. Cole motioned toward Lindsay's laptop all set up on the small wood table. "You're at it early."

"I have to put in my work hours early if I want to get anything done. Reading business material isn't easy to do with the noise of a couple dozen kids barrel racing outside your window." Lindsay tried to sound annoyed, but both Cole and Tizzy noticed the smile on her face. It had only been three and a half weeks and Green Hills was already growing on Lindsay, even she couldn't hide it.

Cole sat down in the third chair with the cup of green tea she had just poured herself. "So we've got two girls down with the flu. Ruthie is taking care of both of them, and we have one camper with a sprained ankle from the mountain biking class yesterday."

"That's okay," Tizzy interrupted, "we'll just put her on the kayaks for the rest of the session."

"Great idea, Tiz." Cole smiled down at her niece. "We're almost done with this first group. Just a couple of more days to go and then only four more sessions." Cole took a sip of her tea to test the temperature.

"Time is flying," Lindsay added. "It seems like with all we have to do around here and the kids keeping us busy, we don't have a minute to rest."

"There's plenty of time to rest in the fall and winter. Mom and Dad mostly just hosted events like conferences and weddings once in a while to help cover the bills in the off season." Tizzy's heart ached every time she mentioned her parents out loud. She thought of them all the time, nonstop some days, but talking about them was harder. The only reason she even brought up her parents now was that she felt the need to convince Cole and Lindsay that the camp could sustain itself, *if* they put in enough hours during the summer. Tizzy looked out the kitchen window as she took a drink of her orange juice.

"I wonder how many kids they have over there." Cole looked at the others for their opinions.

"What?" Lindsay asked. Cole had been a little more spacey than usual since the other day when she had run into Danny at Miller's General Store. Lindsay and Tizzy had no idea where she was going with this change of subject.

"The boys' camp." Cole pointed out the window to where Tizzy had been looking. Three small sailboats with a few boys in each sailed by. They were going at a quick pace in the early-morning mist with a man in a small motor boat keeping up alongside them, giving them directions.

"A lot I bet," Lindsay replied. "I talked with Ruthie about the camps on each side of us, and she said both are doing quite well. Still Waters is full up all summer, and they charge a premium. I guess they would have to with all their buildings and equipment and boats being *brand new*." Lindsay emphasized the last words to bring comparison to their camp, which seemed to be running on fumes. "Which reminds me, Tizzy said that we need to have the north fence checked out and repaired. I'll just add it to my growing list of things that are falling apart around here."

Cole gave Lindsay a warning look that told her not to talk about these things in front of Tizzy. "Tiz, what do you know about the horse camp next door?" Cole asked, redirecting the conversation.

"Not much really. They just opened last year, and the owner and the campers stuck to themselves all last summer. So far, this year it's the same. They specialize in hunter/jumper equitation, and Mom said they were drawing girls from all over the United States. They had some special trainer come give clinics last summer. I think he was in the Olympics or something."

"The Olympics?" Lindsay wailed. "Oh come on, how can we compete with that?"

"We don't have to, Lindsay. We teach barrel racing here, not show jumping. That's a different type of camp." Cole gave Tizzy a secret smile when Lindsay rolled her eyes and got up to refill her coffee cup for the third time.

"I'm just saying they can charge more when they have an Olympian giving clinics," Lindsay said.

It was Cole's turn to roll her eyes so only Tizzy could see. "We don't need to charge more, Lindsay. All we need is a full roster of kids, and we'll be just fine. The last three sessions aren't quite filled to the max. We need to draw in more kids, and I know just how we're going to do it."

"Oh really?" Lindsay looked skeptical. She was used to being the marketing genius, but at this point, she could use some help.

"Yeah, it came to me this morning. The other day, I ran into the operator of Still Waters, Danny Greene. He said his sister used to come here when they were younger, and he always wished he could come too. Anyways, it made me think of all the girls that have come here over the years. I bet they would send their kids and their friend's kids in a heartbeat. We just need to contact them and give them a last-minute discounted summer rate. If we can fill the last few sessions this summer, I think we'll be just fine," Cole finished in a flurry, and a smile spread across her freckled face.

"We're already almost through with this session. That means we only have a little over a week before we need new campers to fill some empty spots. That's sort of short notice," Lindsay seemed skeptical.

"It might work for some of the local kids that don't have any other plans yet. We have to try," Cole replied.

"We'll call them all. Today!" Tizzy's eyes sparkled with the hope of a full camp. "Mom always said our camp isn't about having the best *things*. It's about having the best adventure. We can still give that to each camper. Please, Lindsay," she begged, "let's just try."

"Okay. It's a good idea. There's no harm in trying, right? Let's call Ruthie and have her bring up all the old files." With the decision made, Lindsay rose to fill up her favorite green mug with coffee again. It was going to be a long day.

Chapter 5

"It worked!" Tizzy shrieked after Lindsay announced that they had received their last reservation call only two days after contacting all of the camp alumni. They had completely filled the final three sessions of the summer. Lindsay hugged Tizzy, noticing that the smile on the young girl's face was similar to that when she was riding Sprint, as if she felt pure joy. It was a rare sight.

"I know, I still can't believe it. I'm sort of shocked that that many people would sign up so late." Lindsay pulled her short blonde hair out of her face. "I guess a discount always helps."

Lindsay and Tizzy were standing out on the back porch facing the water. The Sound was calm for a mid-July day. They could see Cole down below taking a group of campers out in the kayaks. "This means we can stay open right?" Tizzy asked.

"For now, yeah." Lindsay smiled gently down at Tizzy. She didn't want to get the girl's hopes up. She knew that Tizzy had some idea of the camp's financial problems, but she wasn't sure yet if she grasped the fact that neither Cole nor Lindsay had committed to staying on the island after summer was over. It had been over a month now, and they still hadn't brought up the Evergreen Boarding School. Lindsay felt bad about not being completely honest with Tizzy, but she didn't even know how she herself felt. There were surprising moments when she loved being back home.

"You know what I love about this place, Tiz?" Tizzy looked up at her aunt. She had a wistful tone to her voice, which was rare for Lindsay. She was usually all business. "I love the fresh air. I love the view of the water and the mountains beyond. In New York, it doesn't smell like this." Tizzy laughed at the thought of Lindsay enjoying this place for the smell of it. "It smells like car exhaust. And hot dogs." At that, Lindsay leaned into Tizzy, and they both began to giggle.

*****

"Oh my gosh, Tizzy, I miss you so much." Ashton sounded homesick.

"I miss you too, Ash. How's Quebec?"

"C'est bien."

"Huh?" Tizzy laughed at Ashton's funny accent.

"It's fine. My mom has Jake and me taking French lessons. Can you believe it? We have to take French lessons…during summer break…while on vacation!" The annoyance made Ashton's voice grow loud. "Jake doesn't even want to do anything now that we're here. He just sits in the house and plays his Xbox, which he just 'had to bring.' So I'm stuck exploring the neighborhood by myself. Which is fine, I guess. It's not the same as being home, though."

"Well, don't worry. You'll be home soon, right? Just another month or so. Then we can go riding together. Pepper is getting restless. I've been trying to ride him lots, but I can tell he misses you." Ashton's small roan gelding Pepper was boarded at the camp barn. "I'm excited for you to meet Cole and Lindsay too. You're going to love them."

"I'm sure I will. Have they said anything yet about staying in the fall?"

"Not yet, but I can tell they love it here. I think they just need more time."

"Well, I'm sure they'll come to their senses and see how awesome the camp is and never want to leave. I, on the other hand, can't wait to get back *as soon as possible*. Maybe we can leave Jake here in Canada." Tizzy and Ashton laughed and said good-bye.

*****

Ruthie stood in the big kitchen of the clubhouse boiling spaghetti noodles and stirring the sauce with a wooden spoon. She could hear the campers playing capture the flag in the big yard out front. It was a sound she had enjoyed listening to for years. "Here, Cole, help me set the buffet table." Ruthie handed her a salad bowl. "It's almost time for dinner."

Ruthie and Cole set out all the food on the red checkered tablecloth that covered the long serving table. "I wonder how many meals I've eaten in here," Cole murmured as she looked around the rustic room.

"Too many to count." Ruthie smiled. "Your mom and dad had you eating here at every meal in the summertime."

"It was a great way to grow up," Cole thought out loud. "I can see why Ann decided to keep it going and raise Tizzy here. Sometimes the memories seem almost too good to be true."

Ruthie paused in the middle of setting out the plates and turned to Cole, "How come you left and moved so far away? Lindsay I can understand. She got a high-power job in a big city, but you could've stayed. I've always wondered why you left." Cole sensed that Ruthie almost took it personally that she had not wanted to stay on the island forever.

Cole looked out the window. "I don't know, Ruthie. It just felt like it was time to see something different, a part of the world I didn't feel comfortable in. Do you ever feel like that?"

"Honestly, hon? No. I like being comfortable right here." Ruthie patted the table for emphasis and laughed at this girl she loved like a firstborn child.

"Once I graduated college, I felt like I needed to do something on my own. It just worked out that I found a place in Nevada that suited me. To be honest though, it never really felt like home. I've lived there for twelve years now, and it still doesn't always feel like it fits me."

"Well, you know where you'll always belong. Green Hills has a way of staying in your blood." Ruthie gave Cole's arm a little pat and then went outside to ring the bell for dinner.

Chapter 6

"Get up!" Tizzy gently squeezed her calves, and Sprint took off around the first barrel without so much as a blink. Leaning into the curve, Tizzy could feel the rush of wind blow the braid off her back. This was her favorite part of the day. She often practiced the barrels after her morning ride. It was a quiet time out at the barn, and she like to get her practice in before everyone was up and wanted to watch. She hadn't competed this last spring like she normally would have. She hadn't wanted to do it without her parents. The San Juan County Rodeo was coming up at the end of summer though, and she had decided that if the camp was going to stay open, she would be back in the circuit.

It was time, she thought, and her parents would have wanted her to.

Tizzy urged Sprint on with her voice and a small nudge. They took the last two barrels and galloped back across the line. Tizzy pulled him up at the fence and spun him around. Just as she turned, she saw something flash through the woods. Squinting her eyes against the rising sun, she scanned the trees but found nothing.

"Hello?" she called. There was no answer. "Must have been a deer." Tizzy muttered to herself, but a nagging feeling told her it was something more.

*****

Miller's Hardware and General Store was crowded with its usual morning coffee customers. In addition to selling just about everything anyone on the island would need, they had a coffee counter in the corner. The same regulars showed up every morning to discuss the local news and whatever else crossed their minds. Cole idled up to the counter and grabbed a cup of tea while she waited for Joe, the manager, to check on a camp order she had placed for some new life jackets.

"Hey, Cole, how are you doing?"

Cole turned at the now familiar voice and smiled when she saw Danny, Still Waters' camp manager. They had met here often, both in on business or just grabbing a cup of coffee and usually stopped to chat. They had a lot in common, each of them being new at running summer camps. Danny, however, seemed to be a natural fit, whereas Cole still wondered if she was cut out for it. "I'm great, Danny, how are you?"

"Fine, just came in for a quick break. Those boys have me out on the water every second of every day. Not that I'm complaining, but sometimes, it's just nice to stretch your legs on land."

Cole smiled at him, and they grabbed a seat together at a window table. "I see you rode your bike in." She nodded toward his mountain bike he had leaned against a bike rack out front.

"Yeah, I've been trying to do some more riding so I don't get rusty and lose all my skills."

"What do you mean skills? I thought you just rode for fun and as a way to get to Millers for a semi-okay cup of coffee," she teased.

"Oh, I do ride for fun, but I was a biker before I ever became a sailor. I grew up going to sailing camp every summer while my sister got to go to Green Hills." Cole could tell he would have preferred to have taken his sister's place. "But growing up in Montana, I rode my mountain bike all year long. I actually competed for a while and did pretty well."

"Really?"

"Yeah, it's sort of my first passion."

An idea sprung into Cole's head and was out of her mouth before she could even fully think it through. "Would you be interested in giving a clinic at Green Hills? We have an awesome mountain biking trail that runs the whole length of the property in back. We used to have a coach that came out every summer, but he moved down south. This year, we've just been getting by. It would be great if we could do some sort of clinic or class. We would pay you, of course."

"Sure, I would love that," Danny answered immediately. His dark eyes crinkled at the edges as he smiled. "I finally found my way into Green Hills Adventure Camp," he teased. "It only took me thirty years."

*****

"You did what?" Lindsay asked, louder than she meant to.

"I asked him to give a private clinic." Cole responded defensively. "I thought it would help us compete with our neighbors, the European Riding Academy." She said their name in a fake snobby English accent, imitating the headmaster she had met just last week. Cole and Lindsay had gone over there the other day to introduce themselves and hadn't even made it inside the front gate. Alberta Highland had been out front of the camp with her assistant, overseeing workers that were trimming the privacy hedge that bordered the camp. They could see campers down the lane walking around in groups, all wearing matching riding blazers with the camp logo on the front. The place smelled of money and confidence. Needless to say, Alberta Highland, the camp headmistress, had not been overly friendly. She had said a quick, "How do you do?" and then dismissed them saying she was on her way to oversee a jumping class. "I know Danny isn't an Olympian or anything, but he sent over his resume, and he has won some big competitions. We can advertise it to the community and try to bring in more business for next year. If it goes well, we could even see if he'd be willing to make some sort of commitment to doing weekly classes with our campers. We have to focus on building this place up if we're going to keep up with our neighbors." Cole seemed to have her argument all mapped out.

"Build this place up?" Lindsay asked, then sat down at the kitchen counter with a thump. "Cole, we haven't even decided if we're staying. They're expecting me back in New York in six weeks!"

"I know that was the original plan, Lindsay, but we have to keep our options open."

"I don't have any options, Cole," Lindsay's voice grew quiet and she shook her head sadly. "I have a job in New York. That's where my life is."

"Life changes all the time, Lindsay. We weren't responsible for a twelve-year-old girl until just a few months ago. Sometimes it's time to make a new plan."

"This just isn't what I had thought this year would look like. I never thought I'd come back here. It's such a small town. I always felt like there was nowhere for me to grow. Definitely not a place where I can run a big marketing firm." Lindsay sighed and hung her head. "Then Chandler and I broke up. I wasn't expecting that either. I should have, though. We barely talked with the time difference. It just seems like everything is falling apart." Lindsay's shoulders slumped.

Cole put her arm around her little sister. "Sometimes things have to fall apart so you can build up something new. Something greater than before."

"I'll think about it," Lindsay promised. She wasn't ready yet to make any decisions about the future of the camp. At this point, she felt like it was just barely hanging on, and so was she.

Chapter 7

"Hey! Hey, you! Stop right there!" Tizzy yelled at the dark-blue blur that was running away from her and into the woods. "This is private property!" she shrieked.

Tizzy kicked Sprint into a quick lope and started gaining on what she could now tell was a teenager wearing a navy-blue sweater with some sort of white logo on the back. It looked familiar, but she couldn't quite place where she had seen it before. The boy was wearing a dark baseball cap and running like his life depended on it. Sprint jumped a fallen tree that had slowed the boy down as he crawled over. "Hey, I said stop!" Tizzy yelled. She caught up with the runaway and circled around to block his path.

The kid bent over, putting his hands on his knees and breathing hard. "Okay, I'm sorry. I'm sorry." He looked up, and Tizzy was surprised to see it was a girl, not a boy, under the baseball cap.

"What are you doing here?" Tizzy stayed mounted on Sprint so she would have the upper hand in case the girl tried to escape.

"I'm sorry, I didn't really think I was doing anything wrong." The girl looked upset, Tizzy thought. She looked closer at the girl's sweater and saw that what she had thought was a logo was actually the European Riding Academy's school crest.

"Are you spying on us?" Tizzy couldn't believe it. She knew the neighbors were snotty, even mean. She had seen some of their girls out riding on the county road, and they had teased her, yelling at her that she looked like a hillbilly on that "splotchy" horse. Tizzy hadn't even wasted her breath correcting them that not only was this "splotchy" horse a three-time junior barrel racing state champion but also that paint horses were regarded as the breed that settled the West, the very land that they were currently riding their expensive thoroughbreds on. Even so, Tizzy couldn't imagine that Alberta Highland would send girls over to spy on the competition. Besides, at this point, even Tizzy had to admit that Green Hills Adventure Camp wasn't much competition, especially to a place like the European Riding Academy.

"No! Well, sort of." The girl reached up and pulled off her baseball cap. Curly blonde hair spilled out from underneath it. She had obviously tucked her hair up into the hat to disguise herself. The girl wrung her hat in her hands, nervous about being caught. "I'm Danielle. I'm so sorry, so, so, sorry. I didn't mean to bug you,"—Danielle seemed flustered—"or spy. I just saw you riding your horse a couple of weeks ago while a group of us were riding out on the ivy path. The other girls were making fun of you"—she looked up at Tizzy who was glaring down at her—"saying your horse looked like a cowboy horse from the old movies. I think he's beautiful, by the way. I've always wanted a paint." Tizzy saw a moment of excitement cross Danielle's face as she looked Sprint over. She even dared to reach out and hold her palm out for Sprint to smell her, but Tizzy didn't give her the chance. She quickly jerked back on the reigns, so Sprint backed up a few steps.

"Why did you come here?" Tizzy asked again.

"I wanted to see your horse again. I've always wanted to ride Western, but my parents never let me. They said it wasn't proper for a young lady. My mom's got this crazy idea that I need to grow up like Scarlett O'Hara. She's like some old-fashioned Southern lady. I'm surprised they don't make me ride side saddle." Danielle tried to laugh but stopped when she saw Tizzy was still frowning. "Anyways, I just wanted to see what it was like over here. I'm stuck next door at the riding academy while my parents travel all over Europe for the summer. They made me sign up for all four sessions, but it was either this or jogging camp." Danielle looked down at her feet and held out her arms to show her slightly out of shape physique. "Can you believe it? Jogging camp?" Danielle had stepped forward again and was stroking Sprint's neck. "What's his name, by the way?"

"Sprint. My mom and dad gave him to me a couple of years ago."

"I heard you do barrel racing over at this camp. That's another reason I came by the other week. I wanted to see what the set up was." Tizzy thought back to the other morning when she was sure she had seen someone watching her practice the barrels. "I've never actually been to a rodeo, but I've always wanted to go. I have a friend back home that went to one once. She had to travel all the way to Ohio, can you believe it? Apparently, they don't have rodeos in Boston. Anyways, it sounded awesome, and I've always wanted to see one myself. I thought this might be the closest thing to seeing a rodeo I'll ever manage. I'm sorry if I caused any trouble."

She didn't look very sorry, Tizzy thought. She just seemed excited to have gotten this close to a "real cowboy horse," and any discomfort she had, she covered up with her talking. Tizzy had never met someone who talked so fast. Maybe it was just because she was nervous. Every part of her seemed to be in constant motion: her hair bounced; her hands bounced; even her cheeks bounced as she talked.

"Since I'm over here, can I see you run the barrels?" Danielle asked.

"No!" Tizzy shook her head. "I mean, we already worked out today. I don't want to overdo it. We're trying to get back in shape for competition in the fall. We took a little time off the last few months." Tizzy hoped she wouldn't have to explain why she had taken a break from riding.

"Well, I get free time every morning before breakfast at 8:00. How about tomorrow?" Danielle looked up at Tizzy, still mounted on Sprint, with such hope in her eyes that Tizzy found it hard to still be mad at her intrusion. Danielle seemed pushy, but Tizzy couldn't imagine being forced to only ride English when she dreamed of riding Western or having parents who sent her off to camp for a whole summer while they left the country. She sort of felt sorry for her.

"Sure, fine." Tizzy rolled her eyes. What was she getting herself in to? "I practice every morning at seven, before the other campers get up. You can watch, but that's it. I don't let anyone else ride Sprint, so don't even get your hopes up," Tizzy warned.

"Great, I'll see you tomorrow morning, 7:00 sharp!" Danielle saluted Tizzy and turned to walk off. "Oh, hey"—she turned back around—"what's your name?"

"It's Tizzy."

"Perfect. Tizzy," she said, trying it out, "Tizzy the cowgirl."

Oh great, Tizzy thought, she just made friends with a city girl, worse yet, a city slicker who loved the idea that Tizzy was a cowgirl. She wasn't a cowgirl. *Well, not really,* she told herself. She did ride Western, and she did wear a cowboy hat in competitions. *I guess in comparison to next-door our camp must feel like the Wild West, outhouses and all.* Tizzy laughed to herself, but while she was giggling, a knot grew tight in the pit of her stomach. For some reason, she felt like she had just opened a can of worms. She watched Danielle walk toward the fence at the northern end of the property. When she got there, she grabbed the two pieces of wire fencing and separated them so that she could crawl through, leaving the wires bent in place where she had stretched them. Tizzy desperately hoped she wouldn't regret inviting her back.

Chapter 8

It was the week between camp sessions. *A much needed week,* Tizzy thought as she flopped down on her bed and turned her iPod volume up. It was always nice to have the place to themselves again. She loved living on a camp, and she loved having groups of different kids come through Green Hills, but she also loved the in-between weeks when it was just her and her family and her horses. Pip jumped up onto the quilt next to her, resting her chin on Tizzy's shoulder. "Hey, girl," Tizzy ran her hand over Pip's head. She thought back to the day she got Pip. It was funny how certain memories just popped into her head. It seemed to happen a lot lately, especially when it was quiet.

It was just last summer, and Tizzy's birthday was at the end of August, so her mom and dad always threw her a big celebration after all the campers had gone home. They had told her to invite some friends over, but Ashton was out of town, and she couldn't really think of anyone else she had wanted to invite. Tizzy remembered the long conversation this led to with her parents, with her complaining that her whole life had been one series after another of different kids coming and going. Of course, she had friends, but not any really close friends besides Ashton. She didn't have time to have friends. She worked all summer at camp and trained all year on Sprint for barrel racing competitions. She hadn't really meant to complain, but sometimes, she just got tired of it all.

Now looking back, she wished she hadn't taken it out on her parents. What had she been thinking? Growing up at Green Hills Adventure Camp was a dream come true. Not just for her, she knew most any kid would say the same. Tizzy couldn't help but feel that life was unfair. There was so much to regret when you can't take back the things you've said. "Even worse"—she looked over at Pip and stroked her head—"is when you don't have the chance to tell the people you love the things you wished you had said more often."

Tizzy rolled over onto her back, and Pip gave a friendly growl, warning her to not stop petting her. "Ok, bossy," Tizzy teased her. At least, that conversation with her parents had resulted in them giving her Pip for her birthday. She had come in from riding

Sprint that morning, and Pip had been sitting in the kitchen with a lime-green bow tied to her collar.

"Happy birthday, Tizzy girl!" They had shouted in unison when she walked in the door. They told her they understood there were some downfalls to living on a camp, but they wanted her to know that they loved her and would always be there for her. Pip would be too.

Well, at least she still had Pip, and now she couldn't be more thankful that her parents had found a way to give her a best friend. It's almost as if they knew she would need one just a short year later.

This summer things seemed to be changing fast, Tizzy thought, but Mom and Dad would be proud that she had finally made a real friend. Danielle had been coming over every morning to watch Tizzy practice the barrels on Sprint. Tizzy had told Cole and Lindsay about what, or more truthfully, who, had been bending the fence. They agreed it was okay for the girl to come over and watch as long as the European Riding Academy allowed them the free time. Lindsay had even gone so far as to call over to the European Riding Academy, or ERA as she was informed by the receptionist, and asked to speak with Alberta Highland, the headmistress. When, after being on hold for five minutes, her assistant informed Lindsay that Ms. Highland was too busy to speak with her, Lindsay had muttered, "Forget it." If one of their girls wanted to escape that horrible camp, well, at least she had tried to warn them.

Ruthie had been brewing coffee in the kitchen where she couldn't help but overhear Lindsay's phone call.

Although Ruthie's back was turned to her, Lindsay could hear her say under her breath, "Heavens to Betsy, I would run away from that lady too." Lindsay laughed as she watched Ruthie wipe her hands on the blue checkered dishcloth and pour two large cups of coffee.

*****

"These trails are incredible," Danny said as he walked the mountain biking grounds with Cole and Lindsay. "Whoever built these knew what they were doing."

"I think Jack, our sister's husband, had really put a lot of work into the trails. It didn't look like this when we were growing up. It was much smaller then." Cole had mentioned the car accident to Danny the last time they met while they were putting up advertisements for the camp. He had asked how long she and her sister were planning on staying on Orcas Island and she had ended up telling him the whole story, all about how uncertain their futures were. More than she thought she would share with someone she just met, but he was so easy to talk to.

"Well, this will definitely do for an amazing clinic." Danny scanned the hills, and Cole smiled at the praise he gave their camp grounds. She looked over at Lindsay and could tell she was pleased too. This was turning out to have been a great idea. "I know I have at least six boys coming over from Still Waters for the clinic."

"That's great," Lindsay sounded excited. "We've had seven other kids call in a reservation, which puts us at thirteen. I know Tizzy will want to do it. So that's at least fourteen kids in the class, and most of them will bring parents or friends to watch." Lindsay turned to Cole. "That's great exposure for us." Lindsay had taken on the marketing for the camp. It was a challenge she seemed to fully enjoy.

"Alright well, all we'll need is to have at least fourteen of your bikes set up and ready to go tomorrow morning. I'll be riding my own bike over. Make sure all the kids and parents sign a safety waiver. That's pretty much it. I've written out a lesson plan and know what skills and tricks I want to go over." Cole was impressed with how seriously Danny was taking the clinic, especially for how last minute they had asked him to do it. "I'm sure I'll have to break up the kids into a couple of different skill levels, so it would be helpful if you guys could be around to help monitor the groups."

"Of course," the sisters said in unison. Cole wasn't going to miss watching Danny ride for anything, and Lindsay wouldn't miss the opportunity to talk up the camp to all the onlookers. The three of them went over some last-minute details and then said good-bye, saying they would see each other bright and early the next morning. Danny took off on his silver mountain bike through the wooded trails that headed south and would eventually lead him to his own camp.

"If I didn't know better, I would say someone has a crush on our next-door neighbor," Lindsay teased Cole.

"He's nice, that's all." Lindsay gave Cole a skeptical look. "Oh, come on, Lindsay, we have a niece and a camp to worry about. I think that's enough for one summer." But Lindsay could see that there was more to it than that, and Cole's blushing cheeks gave her away.

Chapter 9

"Okay, try to relax in the saddle," Tizzy instructed Danielle. After a week of constant begging, Tizzy had finally given in and saddled up Peaches, an old buckskin mare that moved slower than a slug in a pool of marshmallow cream. She thought Peaches might be just the perfect equine match for Danielle. For all of her new friend's excitement and constant jitteriness, she needed a horse that would complement her and balance her out. Tizzy had a gift for matching horses and their riders, a gift that came in handy when saddling up young campers for their first time around the barrels. Her dad had always relied heavily on this ability for the safety of the campers, knowing that Tizzy would never put a girl on one of the more advanced horses if she wasn't ready. Tizzy knew that Peaches was calm enough to help Danielle learn Western riding from the ground up without being affected by the girl's eagerness, which often came across as non-stop energy. That was something that a horse could definitely sense and cause to become anxious. What else made Peaches a perfect match for Danielle was that being a buckskin, a light-brown almost blonde color with a perfect white star on her face, gave her the perfect "cowgirl" look that Tizzy knew Danielle would fall for.

"This ain't my first rodeo," Danielle yelled across the arena to her in her best Western accent.

"Actually it is," Tizzy yelled back in turn and rolled her eyes. Tizzy stood in the middle of the round sand arena and put her hands on her hips. "Western is a lot different than English riding. It's more relaxed. It's less about controlling the horse and more about being in unison with your horse, working together."

"I'm pretty sure that's exactly what I'm trying to do," Danielle snapped back. They had been at it for the last forty-five minutes, and they had just barely gotten Danielle to jog Peaches around the ring. Danielle had bounced around in the saddle so much that Tizzy had her bring the horse quickly back down to a walk. "You're going to give her back pain at that rate. Like I said, you need to relax. It's called Western pleasure for a reason." Tizzy tried to hide her grin as Danielle tried again to jog Peaches, resulting in her bouncing around like she was on a pogo stick.

"I can't believe how different this feels from how we have to ride over at ERA. Headmistress Highland runs the place like we're navy seals. 'Sit up straight, chin up, reins taut,' Danielle mimicked Alberta Highland's deep growl of a voice. "She says the European Riding Academy stands conveniently for ERA because the camp is breeding a new 'era' of young champion equestrians who are, in her words, 'better than the rest.'" Danielle used air quotes and rolled her eyes as she explained the camp's nickname. "Can you believe that stuff? The crazy thing is, Headmistress Highland and some of the campers actually buy into it. She didn't even say we were necessarily better equestrians, just better than everyone else in general. It's hard work to not get caught up in the ridiculousness of it all. It's just that it's everywhere," she said as she pointed down at the embroidered logo on her sweater, which had ERA with a crown above it. "It's like we're supposed to act like we're royalty," she said as she puffed her cheeks out in exasperation. Turning to face Tizzy, Danielle relaxed her shoulders and brought Peaches to a halt. A small smile blossomed on Danielle's rosy face as her mind switched gears back to the present. "By the way, Tizzy, where'd you learn to barrel race?"

"My dad taught me." Tizzy had told Danielle about her parent's accident at the beginning of their lesson. Danielle had asked a million questions, not giving Tizzy the option of keeping it a secret. Tizzy liked Danielle, but sometimes, she needed a break from hearing her nonstop chatter, so she had answered her questions just to hear her own voice for a change. "My mom and dad put me up on a horse before I could walk. They also had a child's seat mounted on the back of their mountain bikes, and we would ride all over the island. My dad wanted me to grow up to be fearless, and he said the way to make that happen was to have me grow up doing things that other people were afraid of. That way, it wouldn't even cross my mind to be afraid of them."

"That's awesome!" Danielle took her eyes off of the back of Peach's ears and looked over at Tizzy in awe. "I so wish my parents were like that. You are so lucky!" The second she said it, she wished she could take it back. Here she was, complaining about her parents, and Tizzy didn't even have parents anymore. Danielle looked at Tizzy and could tell that her comment had stung. "Oh my gosh, I'm so sorry. I didn't mean anything by it."

"It's okay. It's no big deal." Tizzy brushed it off and told Danielle to try to get Peaches to jog again. Deep inside though, Tizzy wondered if she would always be "the girl who lost her parents." Is that how everyone would see her when she went back to school in the fall? Would everyone be weird around her forever, always feeling sorry for her? Tizzy didn't know if she would be able to stand that.

"It's just my parents are so busy trying to get me to be some sort of socialite. They would die if they ever caught me barrel racing," Danielle explained.

They would die if they could see their daughter bouncing around up there like she was on a trampoline,

Tizzy thought. Danielle's parents have probably spent a fortune on riding lessons at some fancy school back in Boston, and she still couldn't ride to save her life. No wonder the girl was miserable.

"And I don't even think they know what mountain biking is," Danielle snorted, laughing and bouncing her way around the arena. "All I meant to say is, your parents sound like they were awesome." Danielle reined Peaches in to a stop and looked over at Tizzy, hoping she took that the right way.

"They were." Tizzy walked toward Peaches as Danielle dismounted and grabbed the reins when she reached them. "See you tomorrow," she said as she quickly turned and led the mare back into the barn leaving Danielle standing in the middle of the arena.

*****

Tizzy couldn't get what Danielle had said out of her head. She brushed Peaches and turned her out into the pasture and then put Sprint in the cross ties in the hallway of the barn. She was giving him a good grooming and working on combing out his main until it shined.

Was she lucky? She couldn't help but think that she wouldn't call it luck to have your parents die when you are only twelve. But then, she also knew that not everyone had parents like hers—parents who taught you how to do amazing things like mountain bike and race horses and parents who took you canoeing every weekend to one of the islands off shore. By rais-

63

ing her on a camp and teaching her how to be brave and adventurous, they had taught her to be confident in herself, to be able to handle difficult situations and still prevail. Sure, life hadn't been perfect. She was beginning to realize that nothing really was, but it had been an adventure, an amazing, awesome adventure. Tizzy started to braid Sprint's main into a perfect French braid, just like her mom had done to her hair and wondered if life could still be. She wasn't so sure anymore.

Chapter *10*

"Hey! Your dog dropped his ball over here!" a boy with cropped hair yelled at Tizzy. The Still Waters swimming area was set up within a hundred yards of Green Hills' beach and dock, and Pip often wandered over there to explore. The boy picked up the sand-covered tennis ball and started walking toward her. Tizzy had come down during the free session in the afternoon when the campers could choose what activity they wanted to do. She usually spent that time in the barn, but it was unusually hot today, so she had decided to take Pip down to the water. The poor dog's long hair didn't do much to help keep her cool, and she loved to splash in the Puget Sound.

"Oh, thanks! You can just throw it."

The boy kept walking toward her anyways, keeping the ball at his side as Pip ran out into the water, chasing a dragonfly. *Great, thanks for keeping me company, Pip,* Tizzy thought. She sat down in the sand and waited for the boy to reach her.

"Cool dog." He stood next to Tizzy and handed her the tennis ball. "I've never seen a small dog that fast before."

Tizzy noticed that the boy had a scar running from the bottom of his nose to his upper lip. She tried not to stare, but he caught her looking at it and put his hand up to cover it self-consciously. Tizzy quickly shifted her gaze out to the water at Pip paddling back to shore.

"Her name's Pip. People underestimate her a lot because she's sort of on the small side. She's super fast though, and you should see her jump." Tizzy laughed when Pip's head accidentally dipped below the water, and she snorted hard to clear her nose. "I'm Tizzy, by the way." Tizzy held out her hand like her dad had always taught her to do.

The boy seemed a little surprised by the formal handshake she gave him. This girl was different; he liked that. "I'm Beau." He smiled at her, and she caught herself looking at his scar again.

"It's from a cleft palate. I had to have surgery on it when I was a baby."

Tizzy was embarrassed to have been caught looking. "Oh, I didn't notice," she lied.

"Yes, you did. I saw you staring at it." He didn't seem mad, just matter of fact. "It's okay. Lots of people do."

Tizzy didn't want to be one of those people. Her cheeks flushed red, embarrassed. "Sorry." She looked away and then turned back. If he wasn't shy about it, she wouldn't be either. "What's a cleft palate?"

"I didn't have skin to cover that part of my mouth when I was born. They had to do a surgery to close up the area that was exposed."

"Oh. I've never heard of that before. Does it hurt?" Tizzy knew she shouldn't be asking so many personal questions, especially since she didn't even know him, but he didn't seem to mind.

"No, it's just a scar. Scars don't hurt." He smiled, and this time, Tizzy noticed how his eyes crinkled when he did. "Lots of people have scars. I bet you have a few just from being at that camp this week." Beau motioned up the cliff to Green Hills Adventure Camp.

"Ha! I live here. My parents owned this camp, and yeah, I've got *a lot* of scars, and you're right, most of them have come from this camp." She laughed at the truth of that. "I guess you don't get too many injuries sailing."

"Oh, you can. Sailing can actually be pretty dangerous, but Danny, he runs the camp, is serious about safety. No casualties yet. Well, at least no one has died." Beau laughed out loud at his joke.

"Do you guys ever sail out to the islands?" Tizzy asked and pointed out a couple of the small islands nearby. There were several tiny landmasses that dotted the shore. They weren't far out, and Tizzy and her parents used to canoe or kayak out to them on the weekends. They would bring a picnic lunch and spend the afternoon out on the water.

"No, we're not allowed to get off the boat once we're out on the water." Beau looked as if he wished this weren't the rule. "Have you?"

"Yeah." Tizzy told him all about her parents taking her out there. "See that island?" She pointed far off to the left. "My dad and I flew over it once in a seaplane. It's in the shape of a horseshoe. We used to go out to that island the most. It has a small inlet with a sandy beach, and it's perfect for swimming because the waves don't get too rough." Beau noticed that she was talking about her parents in the past tense.

"Do your parents still take you out there?" he asked her. Although he had heard a rumor amongst the boys at his camp about what had happened to them, he was hoping it wasn't true and that Tizzy would tell him otherwise.

"No, not anymore." She didn't say anything else but instead got up and brushed the sand off her legs. She started to walk back toward camp, but at the last second, she turned around and saw he was watching her. "Nice to meet you, Beau."

"You too."

On her way back up to camp, Tizzy wondered what it would be like if her parents' deaths had left a scar on her that everyone else could see. Would they all ask her about it? Even if the scar was invisible, was it something that would mark her heart forever?

Chapter *11*

"Okay, everyone, line up with your bikes over there at that trail head," Danny's voice boomed out over the students. Parents lined the fence that blocked off the riding area. Lindsay looked around with a huge grin on her face, there must have been at least sixty people there. A lot of the townspeople had come out too. Maybe they just couldn't pass up the opportunity to see what the sisters had done to the camp, but if snooping was all it was, Lindsay didn't care. She wanted interest and publicity, any kind of publicity.

Tizzy was one of five girls who were participating in the clinic. They had been there for a couple of hours already, and things couldn't have been going better, Tizzy thought. Danny had started out the day assessing the riders, putting them in groups according to their skills and experience. Tizzy was in the most advanced group with one other girl and a boy from Still Waters.

She recognized most of the riders from school and around town, but a few of the boys from Still Waters she had never met before. She had noticed right away, however, that Beau, the boy she had met on the beach, was attending and had been placed in the intermediate group. She didn't think he had done a lot of mountain biking before, but he seemed naturally athletic and was getting along fine.

"All right, folks!" Danny got everyone's attention by clapping his hands and then holding them above his head for silence. The audience all quieted down and turned to him. "We're going to end our clinic today with a little show, but first, I want to thank everyone for coming." Danny smiled at the parents, his charisma infecting them all. "We have Green Hills Adventure Camp and Camp Still Waters brochures located over there on the lemonade table. Please help yourself to a refreshment and some of the information packets. And now, for the grand finale." Danny's eyes twinkled as he swung around toward the kids, most of whom were giggling in nervousness at showing off their new skills.

Danny lowered his voice so that only the kids could hear. "All right, guys, I want you all to ride the trail one after the other starting with Tizzy. Give each other a good thirty yards of space before you take off after the person in front of you, and I want you all to do a new trick you learned today. It can be taking one of the larger jumps or a wall ride on the far side of the course, whatever you feel comfortable with." Danny winked at all the campers. "Now go give them a show!" he shouted, and Tizzy took off.

*****

Cole and Lindsay ran up to Tizzy as she skidded to a stop at the end of the trail. "Tiz, you're awesome!" They hugged and squeezed her until Tizzy couldn't help but laugh, only a little embarrassed. *It actually feels good to be fussed over,* she thought. "Thanks, Danny was great. I feel like I learned so much in just one day." Her aunts noticed that Tizzy's flushed cheeks were glowing.

"It was a total success," Lindsay squealed to the other two. "I have to go man the brochure table. I want to make sure that everyone gets a pamphlet." Lindsay hurried off to greet all the parents.

"She seems happy." Tizzy watched her aunt run over to the lemonade table where parents and friends were crowding around, chatting with one another and congratulating campers on their performance.

"She is, I think." Cole put her arm around Tizzy, and they started walking back toward the main house. "This has been a big adjustment for her. She's used to a different way of life, Tizzy. Here's a secret, just between you and me, your mom and I always knew Lindsay would leave here. Even when we were little, she just seemed like she was almost *too big* for this island." Tizzy and her aunt stopped and looked back at Lindsay, decked out in cowboy boots and a blue bandana holding back her bangs, handing out flyers and shaking hands. "It was almost like she needed a bigger place so she could grow to her full potential. Neither your mom nor I was surprised when she left at eighteen and went to college in New York. I guess we had seen it coming, and it seemed to make her happy." Tizzy looked at Lindsay, standing there all business and then at Cole, who always seemed content and realized for the first time just how much their lives had changed since her parents died. Cole put her arm back around Tizzy's shoulders and started walking again. "She seems to have fallen in love with this island again, though. At least with a few things here." She gave Tizzy a tight squeeze. "You being the most important." Tizzy felt bubbles in her stomach start to pop when her aunt said that. Life was starting to feel good again. At least on days like this, she thought, and walked up the porch steps to her home.

*****

"See up there, Tizzy?" Cole pointed straight up and slightly over their heads. Tizzy squinted. "See? One, two, three, four." She counted out the stars as she drew the shape of a box. "That's Pegasus. The stars are in the shape of a horse's body."

"Really? That's awesome." Tizzy smiled up at the night sky.

"Pegasus is a white winged horse from Greek mythology," Cole explained. "Those stars were always my favorite."

Tizzy, Cole, and Lindsay had laid out an old green flannel blanket on the grass in front of the house. They all laid back, Tizzy in the middle of her aunts, and folded their hands behind their heads. They were taking turns telling stories. Tizzy realized that this was the first time since her aunts had arrived six weeks ago that they were spending the evening just the three of them, like a family. They had spent a lot of time together since camp had begun, but they were usually working or talking about camp, or Lindsay was on her computer doing work that needed to be sent back to New York ASAP. Tonight, it felt like they were together because they wanted to be. "Which ones are your favorite, Lindsay?" Tizzy asked.

"Hmmm, I always liked the Big Dipper." She laughed quietly. "I think because that was the only one I could ever really find. Cole was always much better at identifying the stars." Lindsay looked over at her sister and laughed. "Remember when Mom and Dad took the three of us on that overnight backpacking trip in the Olympic mountains? We couldn't have been more than what, eight, ten, and twelve years old?" She turned to Tizzy excited to share this story. "Mom and Dad had hiked back to the car, maybe a mile or two away, to get the rain cover because it looked like it was going to rain that night. They had told us to stay at the camp with Cole in charge, as always, because she was the oldest."

Tizzy could tell by the way Lindsay said it teasingly that this used to be an issue between them. "It began raining while they were gone, and Annie started to get scared. I mean really, really scared. She thought we were lost in the woods and began crying, which of course got me scared, and I started crying too. It was such a big mess, but Cole kept her cool." Tizzy looked over at her other aunt and could tell she was trying hard to keep from laughing. "Your mom started to really panic, and I wasn't helping the situation at all by crying myself, so Cole decided we had to go find Mom and Dad.

"She was in the middle of reading this book series about sailors that charted the night sky and was *obsessed* with stars. She told me and your mom that the sailors could always find their way by following the North Star. So we all walked out into a clearing, and Cole found the North Star and pointed it out to us and told us that if we followed it, we would find Mom and Dad. Ann stopped crying, and we all put on our rain jackets and started hiking. Thank God we only got about fifty yards before we heard Mom and Dad behind us asking us where we thought we were going. Annie turned around quickly and shouted, 'It worked! We barely even had to follow the North Star, and we found them!'" Tizzy, Cole, and Lindsay all burst out laughing, grabbing their bellies and covering their mouths to keep the noise down.

When they finally quieted down, Tizzy looked at her aunts. "That must be why the North Star was Mom's favorite."

"It was. Ann always said that the North Star would lead her wherever she needed to go," Cole said softly. "I bet Tizzy, if you look real hard, you can see her up there now." All three of them looked straight up at the star that shined the brightest.

"It makes sense," Lindsay added, "for your mom to be somewhere where you could always find her. She never would've left you, Tizzy, if she'd had a choice." Lindsay reached over and grabbed Tizzy's hand, and within seconds, Cole grabbed her other.

"I like that," Tizzy thought for a moment. "I think that's exactly where she is." Tears started to roll gently down her cheeks, but for the first time, Tizzy didn't feel the deep pain that always came with them.

Chapter *12*

"Tizzy, you should have heard them. It was so obnoxious. They just wouldn't quit talking. It was like 'Rene this, Chelsea that.' They won't stop gossiping about people, it's horrible." Tizzy laughed to herself. If Danielle thought that someone else talked a lot she could only imagine. Tizzy had been giving Danielle riding lessons for almost three weeks now, and to both their surprise, she was really improving. At least she no longer bounced around like a jackhammer. Tizzy had even started her on a pattern around the barrels at a jog. She thought that if she kept practicing, Danielle might actually be able to pull it off. She could actually someday compete. Well, maybe. It would help if she talked less and thought more about what she was doing.

But despite what she originally thought of her, Tizzy liked Danielle. She was genuine and honest, and Tizzy liked that.

"They're always going on about how they're the best riders, which I guess they are," Danielle added in an annoyed voice, "but that's only because their parents can afford to send them to the best trainers." Danielle had been complaining about Sheila for most of the three weeks they'd know each other, but Tizzy agreed she sounded awful. All she knew about Sheila, besides the horrible pranks she played on the other girls at camp, was that she was tall, thin as a rail, and had long wavy blonde hair that didn't curl in a corkscrew like Danielle's but looked instead like she had just stepped off the beach. "Sheila is really at it this week. She even made one of the new girls from this session cry. She told her that her riding breeches 'were knockoffs of some designer brand because her parents couldn't afford the real thing.'" Danielle paused to take a rare breath. "You're lucky you don't live across the water in Seattle, Tizzy, or you might run into her more on the riding circuit. All she can talk about is her blue ribbons, and if she's not bragging about herself, she's being rude to some of the other girls at camp, including me."

Tizzy tried to ignore the gossip. "Okay, run 'em again, Danielle, but this time, try it at a lope. Just keep her nice and steady, and remember to lean into the barrels."

"And she's totally using Amy for her brother. I guess they all go to the same school, and their parents sent them all to camp together for the whole summer. Amy's brother is over at Still Waters. Sheila acts all nice to Amy's face, who's actually pretty nice, but talks behind her back all the time. It's so obvious she's only friends with Amy because of her brother. Apparently, Sheila has a *huge* crush on him. He's some sort of rugby king at their school. The Queen of Mean," Danielle paused and looked over at Tizzy to make sure she was listening, "that's what I'm calling Sheila now, is always going on and on about Beau Mansfield."

"Whoa!" Tizzy called from the rail. Peaches came to an immediate halt, almost sending Danielle flying over his head and into the dirt.

"Hey! You almost killed me! What is it, I thought that was going pretty good."

"Beau? A boy named Beau that's at Still Waters is this girl's brother?"

"Yeah, I guess. What about it?"

"Oh nothing, I just think I might know him." *There can't be two Beaus in one camp,* Tizzy thought. She hadn't told anyone about meeting Beau. There really wasn't anything to tell, but she had been thinking a lot lately about how honest and open he had been with her about his scar and how little it seemed to bother him to talk about something that others might try to hide. Somehow, it seemed to make him stronger, more confident. She liked that about him.

"Okay, sorry, Danielle. Try it again."

Danielle gave Tizzy a funny look and then circled Peaches around. "Whatever you say, boss," she said in a western accent and nudged the mare into a fast lope.

*****

"How're things going with Danielle?" Cole asked when Tizzy walked in the kitchen from her morning lesson. Tizzy looked a little worn out, Cole thought. She was worried that the girl was taking on too much responsibility at the camp, especially since she was still adjusting to life without her parents, not to mention life with her aunts.

"It's fine. I honestly thought there was no hope for her at first," Tizzy gave Cole a guilty-looking smile. "I know, I know, there's hope for everybody on a horse."

"You know where that saying came from?" Cole asked.

"My mom always said that. We would have campers who were amazing mountain bikers and great out on the water but were terrified of horses. Mom always said it was because it was totally out of their control. That with a bike or a boat, you get to decide what happens. But with riding, you have to share the choices with your horse. It's like your horse gets a say too." Tizzy had walked over to the fridge to get the milk. Cole listened carefully to her niece. Tizzy didn't talk about her parents that much, and Cole wanted to make sure Tizzy knew that she would always be there to listen. Reaching into the fridge, Tizzy said, "But Mom would always tell the campers, especially the ones that were hesitant around the horses, 'There's hope for everybody on a horse.'" Tizzy sat back down next to her aunt. "I used to think it was kind of silly, like some old cliché, but I could tell that she always meant it."

Lindsay came into the kitchen from the living room. She looked sleepy and had dark circles under her eyes. "What are you guys talking about?" she asked.

"Well"—Cole smiled at her sister—"I was just going to tell Tizzy that it was *our grandpa* who used to always say, 'There's hope for everybody on a horse.'" Tizzy snapped her head up and looked at her aunt.

"Really?"

"Yeah, so I guess it's actually a family saying. I remember when your mom and Lindsay and I used to go visit Grandma and Grandpa during school breaks. They lived out on a farm in Pomeroy, and Dad and Mom would drop us off out there for a week or so."

"Talk about small towns," Lindsay interrupted and rolled her eyes.

"We had fun, though. That's where we all learned how to ride."

"I thought you learned here at camp?" Tizzy asked.

"No," Cole answered, "the spring before our parents opened up Green Hills, we spent three weeks out at Grandma and Grandpa's farm. It was the first time Ann had been away from home for more than a couple of nights." Cole looked at Lindsay. "She must have been what, five?"

"Yeah, maybe even younger."

"She was homesick for our parents and was having a hard time out there. It was our third or fourth day there and poor Ann had cried most of the night. Grandpa came in the next morning after doing his chores and picked Ann up, saying he had an idea. He swung her up on his shoulders and headed out the screen door. Lindsay and I followed them across the yard to the corral where he kept the most beautiful dapple gray mare."

"Grandma had named her Ellie. She was my first love." Cole and Tizzy laughed at the dreamy look in Lindsay's eyes.

"Anyways," Cole continued, "Grandpa just walked right into the corral, put a halter on Ellie, and then set Ann up on her back. She looked absolutely terrified for about five seconds, and then she had the biggest smile on her face, like she had died and gone to heaven. It totally did the trick. Grandpa walked her around and around that corral with Lindsay and I waiting our turn standing on the fence, and I remember him saying, 'See, girls, there's hope for everybody on a horse. Even a sad little girl that misses her parents.'"

Cole turned and put her hand on Tizzy's. "Thanks," Tizzy whispered, her voice breaking as she held back the tears.

Chapter *13*

Ashton,

I hope you're having fun in Quebec (even if Jake is a total pain!) The island isn't the same without you, but this summer is actually turning out all right, I guess. I can't wait for you to meet my aunts. You're going to love them. The more I get to know them, the more they remind me of my mom. It's kind of hard to see at first, but they all have a lot of the same qualities. Neither of them is the real cowgirl type, at least you wouldn't think so, but

the three of us have been taking
trail rides a lot of nights after
dinner when Ruthie takes over
the campers. You should see us,
me with a hippie and a business-
woman riding the wooded trails.
I feel like we would make a good
reality TV show, ha! They're both
pretty good riders though, for
not having done it in years. And
you should see Lindsay on a bike!
I never would have expected
it, but that is what she says she
loved most growing up here.
She can take some of the most
advanced jumps we have here,
and I think she's having a lot of
fun teaching the campers. It's a
miracle, Ashton, I think they're
both actually liking being back
here. Maybe even loving it.

They still haven't said anything
about what the plan is for the
fall. I *was* worried that they were
going to make me move to one
of their places halfway across the
country. Ruthie had warned me
before they came that it was a
possibility, but I'm beginning to
think they might want to keep
the camp running. Lindsay has

done a lot of work on filling up the empty spots, and we were able to book up the rest of the summer. So who knows? Send prayers my way that they do decide to stay. I don't know what I would do if they sold the camp. This is my home. This is where all my memories are. I *love* this place.

Enough about me, though. Have you been able to do any riding in Quebec? I can't wait for you to come back to Orcas. I still have so much to tell you.

Au revior! (I think that's how it's spelled in French!)

Tizzy

*****

Tizzy crawled under the covers. "Come on, Pip." She patted the bed next to her, and Pip hopped up. The dog circled her usual spot, sniffing the quilt before plopping down on the faded patch next to Tizzy. It had been a long day. Tizzy had woken up early to give Danielle her riding lesson. She was really progressing well and could now take the barrels at a lope. Peaches and Danielle seemed like a perfect fit, and Tizzy's new friend showed an enthusiasm for barrel racing. Now that she was moving a little faster and had to concentrate more, Danielle had even quit talking so much, at least when they were going around the barrels. Spending time with Danielle made Tizzy think a lot about how lucky she was to have had her parents. Sometimes, especially right after the accident, Tizzy hadn't thought of it that way. There had been times when she thought that it might have been better to have had parents who weren't so amazing, then maybe her heart would ache a little less. But hearing about Danielle's parents and how much they didn't seem to understand their daughter or respect what she wanted made Tizzy more grateful than ever. She was beginning to understand that any second spent with her parents had been a blessing. It was something she had known all along, just maybe taken for granted. She wouldn't do that again, she promised herself, and thought of her aunts. Tizzy looked at the picture of her mom and dad on her bedside table. "They're not so bad," she told her parents. "*If* I can't have you guys." Tizzy closed her eyes and fell into the best sleep she had had all summer.

*****

The next morning, the three ladies of Green Hills took their usual places at the kitchen table. The second-to-last session of the summer was winding down.

"Okay, you guys, I have an idea." Lindsay smiled conspiratorially, her eyes bouncing quickly from Tizzy to Cole and back again.

"Uh-oh, what is it?" Cole asked. She had heard her fair share of Lindsay's crazy ideas over the years, and more often than not, they didn't work out. She was still amazed at some of the things she had let her little sister talk her into, like the time they tried to swim out to the little horseshoe island by themselves. Lindsay had just finished reading *Swiss Family Robinson* and had convinced Cole that they could set up a secret camp there. They had almost drowned halfway to the island, and thankfully, a neighbor had been nearby on his boat and had rescued them.

"I want to have an end-of-the-summer multi-camp event." Lindsay was so excited she couldn't sit still. She jiggled her leg up and down and continued to speak, waving her hands in the air as she detailed her idea. "I've been thinking, we have to diversify. We need more exposure, and this will let the kids from Still Waters and The European Riding Academy see Green Hills and find out what we're all about. They'll go home and tell friends and siblings, and if we're still open next summer"—she cast a quick, worried look at Tizzy; she didn't want the girl to get her hopes up—"we might fill up. We could even need to add a session if this really works out."

"What exactly are you planning? What is a multi-camp event?" Cole asked skeptically.

"I want to do our own version of a triathlon."

"A what?" Tizzy asked.

"A triathlon. It's a race where the competitors do three events. It's usually swimming, biking, and running, but I thought we could do a triathlon Green Hills style. And to include the other two camps, we could include their sports too. So I thought we could borrow Still Water's dinghys and sail a quick course then mountain bike the paths out back and finish off with a horseback ride. I'm sure Alberta will make us ride English to finish the race. We could do it on the last day of the next session when all the parents are here to pick up their kids. The last session is the two-week-long camp so they'll have extra time to practice the other events. Plus, it would be *amazing* exposure. What do you guys think?"

"I think it sounds awesome *if* we can pull it off. We only have a couple of weeks till then," Cole voiced.

"We've never done anything like it before." Tizzy saw the sparkle in her aunt's eyes. This was the first time all summer that Lindsay had even mentioned the possibility of the camp still being open next year, and Tizzy grasped at that chance. "I'm in," she said.

"It'll be a lot of work, but I've already started making up the flyers and mailers that we can send out to all the kids' parents. We can even post some at Miller's General Store, the library, and other places around town. I think it's time we got people to see what we're doing here." A huge smile spread across Lindsay's face. It had been easier to convince Cole and Tizzy than she had thought.

"Okay, but let's not tell anybody yet. We have to make sure Danny and Alberta are onboard, and Alberta might be harder to convince than we think." Cole scrunched up her nose. "Who's going to talk to her?"

"I will." Lindsay thought it was only fair since it was her idea that she would have to talk to her. "I'm not looking forward to it, though." Cole and Tizzy laughed at the grumpy face Lindsay was making, grateful they didn't have to be the ones to convince Alberta Highland to join in on their camp spirit.

*****

The rest of the week went by quickly. The campers from this session went home, and Green Hills was empty for a whole week before the last campers of the summer came in. It was the middle of August and hot and humid outside. Tizzy thought she might ride Sprint out on the wooded path behind the camp where it would be cooler. She pulled on her brown leather paddock boots and walked up the driveway from the house to the big white barn. She could see her aunts in the barn, grooming and tacking up two of the horses, but she was still too far away to see exactly what they were doing.

As Tizzy got closer, she saw that they had Scout and Summer in the cross ties. Cole had already put a trick riding saddle on Summer's back, and Lindsay was about to do the same to Scout. "What are you guys doing?" Tizzy asked with an edge to her voice.

Cole and Lindsay heads snapped her way. They hadn't heard her coming. They had been laughing at a story Lindsay was telling about some of her friends back in New York. "If they could see me now," she had said, "about to practice for a summer camp rodeo performance—" but the sharp tone in Tizzy's voice made then stop giggling. "We're just going to practice a little bit on Summer and Scout. We thought that we might do a sort of halftime show after the triathlon, just to show some of the parents what our horses can do."

"I bet none of them have seen much trick riding," Cole added.

"You can't," Tizzy's head jerked away as she said it.

"Why not?" Lindsay asked.

"You can't ride them. They're my parent's horses. I don't want you to ride them." Tizzy had raised her voice as panic set in.

"Tizzy," Cole's voice was soft, trying to calm her niece down, "it's just for the show. We thought it would be a good idea. You've seen us riding Summer and Scout out on the trails."

"These are the best horses we've got besides Sprint," Lindsay added, "and they're our only trick riding horses. If we were as good at barrel racing as you, Tiz, we'd do that, but Cole and I grew up trick riding at rodeos. Your mom was the barrel racer."

"I know that!" Tizzy snapped. "I don't want you to do it. You *can't* do it." The ears of the two horses in the barn hallway swiveled back and forth. They could feel the tension in the air. "Those are my parents' horses, and *you are not* my parents!" Tizzy spun on her heel and ran out of the barn.

When she got back to the house, she stopped and burst into tears. She didn't know why she had acted that way. She wasn't even sure what had caused it. Her aunts were right; she had seen them riding Summer and Scout all summer since they had arrived. She knew those were the horses that they felt most comfortable on, and since they were horses that needed more experienced riders and they didn't usually put campers on them, it had been great that Cole and Lindsay were able to exercise them. Tizzy turned and looked back at the barn. She couldn't see her aunts, but she watched as Summer and Scout left through the barn door and were turned out into the pasture. At least her aunts were respecting her, she thought, although for some reason, getting what she had wanted didn't feel good.

Still crying, Tizzy walked over the lawn toward the bluff. She would head down to the water and think. This didn't make any sense. She and her aunts had been getting along so well. She felt embarrassed about her outburst and even more embarrassed about not even understanding why she felt this way. She didn't know why she didn't want them to perform on the horses. They were right; people would love to see them trick riding on the two beautiful white horses. She knew it would be an amazing performance, and it would probably bring in more business for the camp if they added trick riding to the barrel racing program. Wasn't that exactly what she wanted? To keep the camp running?

Tizzy picked her way carefully down the rocky path that zigzagged down the side of the bluff and led to the dock and private beach that belonged to Green Hills. She could see from up here that the beach was empty. All the counselors usually spent their days off in the small town on Orcas Island, hanging out at the café or at the bigger beach on the south side of the island. Just a hundred yards up the beach though, she could see that the Still Waters' campers were all out basking in the sun. Some of the boys were swimming and splashing around in the water, and a few others were sitting on the dock by the sailboats that were tethered there.

Tizzy kept heading down toward the empty beach just below her. She was thankful for the large area of boulders that separated Still Waters' waterfront from theirs. She would have her privacy, even if the boys could see her, and she needed that. She needed time to think about what had just happened.

For the first time, Tizzy knew that she loved her aunts, and that they had not once acted like they thought they were her parents. All they wanted to do was ride Summer and Scout at the Adventure Triathlon, show off some fancy tricks they remembered from childhood, and—she now realized guiltily—had probably been hard at work practicing. What was it that bugged her so much? Tizzy leaned back on her elbows, resting in the sand and looked out over the dark-gray waters of the Puget Sound.

She squinted against the sun and tried hard to figure out what she was feeling. Then it clicked, just
like that. It was so obvious. It was the finality of it
all that she couldn't stand. Tizzy knew her parents
were gone and that they weren't ever coming back. It
wasn't a problem that her aunts were riding her parent's horses; it was a problem that other people would
see them doing it and not know any different. They
would be trick riding in front of a whole crowd of
strangers who knew nothing about Tizzy or her mom
or her dad. All they would see would be two sisters
who now ran the camp, up there galloping around
the arena on beautiful matching white horses, and
it would be like her parents never existed. Everyone
would just think that the horses had belonged to
Cole and Lindsay their whole life. People would
hear about the sisters having grown up on the island
at the camp, and the whole memory of her parents
would be washed away. Tizzy didn't think she could
stand that. And although she felt sorry for how she
acted with her aunts, she didn't think that they would
understand.

*****

"Hey, Tizzy." Her eyes snapped open, and she
sat up.

Beau stood right next to her, blocking the sun
so that he looked like a big shadow. "Oh, hi," Tizzy
looked down and brushed the sand off her elbows
and hands.

"A couple of us are going to go sailing out on the water. I was wondering if you wanted to come too. Danny said it was okay." Tizzy looked over at the Still Waters' end of the beach and saw Danny smile and wave her on over.

"I don't know." Tizzy hesitated. She had planned on spending some time alone to work out what had just happened with her aunts.

"Come on." Beau reached out his hand to help her up. He had seen her come down the walkway to the beach and lay down. He could tell she was upset about something. She had lain down and not moved for fifteen minutes but didn't look like she was relaxing or enjoying the sun. "It'll be fun. We're planning on exploring some of the islands. Danny said this was the one time we could get off the boats."

At that, Tizzy's eyes brightened. "Okay." She smiled. She hadn't been out to any of the islands all summer, and her parents used to take her out there all the time just to explore or have a picnic. Beau and Tizzy walked back toward the Still Waters dock where all the small sailboats waited.

"Hey, Tizzy"—Danny grinned at her—"glad you're joining us." Tizzy looked around at the five other boys who were preparing the sailboats, and Danny leaned in and whispered, "I already texted Cole and asked if it was okay for you to come. She said no problem." Even though Tizzy was upset with her aunts, she was glad that they wouldn't be worrying about where she was.

"Okay, we're going to go out in groups of two." The boys all began pairing up, and Beau came and stood right next to Tizzy. Danny took a spot next to the last boy. "All right, I want everyone to stay within eyesight of my boat. You can explore either of those two islands." He pointed off shore and to the north. Tizzy already knew where she wanted to go.

*****

"Straight that way," she gave directions to Beau while he did most of the work. "If you just go around the other side of the island, like I told you about, you'll see the beach. I'm pretty sure we'll still be able to see Danny, so it'll be okay." Tizzy felt the wind blowing hard on her face, her long braid whipping at her back. She had never felt so much exhilaration on the water before.

"Okay, I need to pull that rope tight." Beau was a patient teacher, and Tizzy felt like she was starting to get a hang of it as they headed straight toward Horseshoe Island. They couldn't talk much because the thrum of the wind was so loud in their ears, but Beau kept on shouting instructions until Tizzy felt like she was actually pulling her own weight and helping to guide the sailboat. They finally came up on the sandy beach and looked to make sure that Danny could still see them. Two of the other boats had beached on the island just across from them, and Danny and his partner were sailing, practicing turns, between the two groups.

Beau and Tizzy got out and headed toward the dry sheltered beach. Wading through water after jumping out of the boat, Tizzy looked around, familiarizing herself once again with the small island that she had grown up visiting with her parents. "See, this was the cove I told you about," she called out to Beau who was a few yards behind her, securing the boat. "The whole island curves around this beach." It had always been her favorite place to come with her mom and dad.

Tizzy and Beau walked around the beach, looking at starfish and exploring in between the large rocks that dotted the shore. "So how come you seemed upset today? Earlier, when you were back on your beach at camp." Beau was nervous about asking because he was just getting to know her, but something in her eyes had made him worried.

Surprised he asked her such a personal question, Tizzy was about to tell him that it was nothing, but being on this island where she and her parents had spent so much time made her think about his question and answer it honestly. "It's just family stuff." She shrugged her shoulders. "My aunts and I got into an argument." Beau sat down on the sand and turned to face her, listening quietly. After a few moments of silence, Tizzy continued, "Sometimes, I feel like life shouldn't be going on without my parents. I know my aunts are just trying to help, but they're taking over. They're planning this big end-of-summer event and wanted to perform a trick riding show on my parents' horses. They didn't even ask." Saying it out loud, Tizzy realized it sounded a little ridiculous, but Beau just sat there, listening, so she went on. "I know it doesn't sound like a big deal, but when I realized they were planning on riding my mom and dad's horses in the show, it felt like they were trying to take their place in front of everyone. All these people would see my aunts and think that they belonged here." Tizzy looked down at her feet now. "It should be my mom and dad."

Beau looked closely at his new friend. He could see there were tears welling up in her eyes about to spill over and he felt sorry for her. He wasn't sure what to say. He wasn't sure if there was anything he could say to make her feel better. He reached up and rubbed the scar above his lip, a habit he had when he was thinking seriously. "That's hard, Tizzy." He squinted out over the water toward where the two camps were, blinking against the sun. "I've never lost anyone that close to me, so I don't really know what you're going through." Tizzy felt relieved that he wasn't going to tell her he knew just how she felt or what the answer was to all her problems. She didn't think there was one. They sat in silence for a few minutes. Then he spoke quietly, still looking out over the water and still rubbing his scar, "This must be hard for your aunts too, Tizzy. I know sometimes it's hard to see beyond our own grief and our own pain. I *have* felt that before. I do know what it's like to go through something hard that leaves scars, Tizzy, even if it's not losing my parents." She looked over at him, and he put his hands back on the sand, letting his

96

face reflect the sun. She could see the heavy line that ran from his upper lip to his nose, and she wondered what it was like to live with a scar so visible, a scar that everyone saw before they even saw you. "What has happened to you has hurt your aunts too. We've all got scars, Tizzy. It's unfair of you to think you're the only one in your house with one."

Tizzy felt a sting of pain in her stomach. For just a second, she felt angry at him for being so harsh, so honest, but before she could say anything back, there was a little whisper inside her head that told her maybe he was right. She knew her aunts were hurting too, but maybe she had been too blinded by her own pain to really see it.

Both Beau and Tizzy were quiet as they sailed back toward Orcas Island. The only time they talked was when Beau was giving Tizzy sailing instructions, but she wasn't mad at him, and he knew it. She wasn't exactly sure what she felt quite yet, but she knew she was grateful that someone else seemed to understand the scars on her heart.

Chapter 14

"I think she just needs some space. This is still a lot for her to take in," Cole was saying to Lindsay. She was surprised that Lindsay had burst into tears when Tizzy ran away from the barn. Lindsay had always been the strong one. Cole wasn't sure if she had ever seen her cry.

"I know, I know," she muttered as she wiped her eyes with the back of her hand. "It's just so," Lindsay paused, looking for just the right word to explain how awful it was.

"Incredibly horrible," Cole chimed in.

"Yes! The whole things is so incredibly horrible. What happened to Ann and Jack and now not knowing what to do about the camp. And the guilt"— Lindsay's shoulders sagged with grief—"the guilt of not having gotten to know Tizzy sooner." Lindsay's head fell into her hands, and she started crying again.

"I feel the same way. I think we all just got so caught up in our own lives, and you never expect anything like this to happen. I thought we would have forever to come back home and spend more time with Ann and Jack and Tizzy."

"I love her, Cole." Lindsay looked at her sister with wide eyes.

"I know, I do too. She's easy to love." Cole reached across the table and held Lindsay's hand.

"I want to do what's best for Tizzy, I'm just not sure I know what that is." Both girls sat together in silence for a minute. "We each have our own lives already built—mine in New York and yours in Nevada. We don't even know what we're doing half the time here on this island, on this *camp*." Exasperation leaked into Lindsay voice.

"Let's just make it through the summer. We'll focus on one day at a time, making each day the best it can be for Tizzy and for the camp. We don't even know what all our options are yet. Who knows if the camp will even be able to afford to stay open after the summer?"

The kitchen's side door creaked as it slowly opened. Both Cole and Lindsay looked up in time to see Pip slink around the door with Tizzy right behind her. Tizzy slowly came into the room looking embarrassed, Cole thought, even though she had no reason to be. Cole understood that Tizzy's outburst had less to do with her aunts and more to do with all of the confusing emotions she had felt throughout the last several months. It was exhausting, Cole knew, and it might actually do the girl some good to be able to vent her feelings, whether they were anger or frustration, every once in a while.

"Hey," Tizzy whispered, keeping her eyes on the ground where Pip sat next to her. Pip, always aware of Tizzy's feelings, laid a paw on top of Tizzy's Keds. "I'm sorry."

"You don't have to be sorry, honey. It's okay," Cole answered first.

"It's just," Tizzy wasn't sure how to explain it, "I just . . . it was weird thinking about you guys riding Summer and Scout at the end-of-summer celebration. I don't know, it just felt like it was something that my mom and dad should be doing. It's something that they *would be doing* if they were still here." Cole and Lindsay could see how hard it was for Tizzy to explain this to them.

"You don't have to worry about hurting our feelings, Tiz." Lindsay reached up and put her hand on Tizzy's shoulder. "You're right. This is something that your mom and dad should be doing. They should be here. I would give anything for them to be here with us. I wish I could promise to make this all better, Tiz, to make things the way they were, but I can't. All I can guarantee is that Cole and I would never mean to do anything to hurt you, Tizzy, or to make you feel like we're trying to take your parents' place."

"I know," Tizzy said, and she did. She knew her aunts hadn't meant to replace her parents, but it still felt unfair. It should have been her mom and dad, but now, knowing that was impossible, she realized that the next best thing she could do was save the camp, if not for herself, then for her parents. If having her aunts put on a trick riding show would bring in more interested campers and possibly help her do just what she wanted to do, she wouldn't stand in their way. "I want you to ride them. I want you guys to do the trick-riding exhibition." Tizzy looked up to the shelf in the kitchen that held a framed photo of her and her parents on a trail ride when she was eight. "I want this to be the highlight of the summer."

"It will be. *That* I can promise," Lindsay said with relief and determination while she stood up. "In that case, I've got work to do." She walked over to the coffee pot and poured a third cup, came back to the table, and grabbed her laptop on her way to the office. As she walked away, she stopped, turning back to face Tizzy and Cole, "We're going to make this work. I'll meet you in the barn in fifteen minutes."

"Uh-oh." Cole laughed and looked at Tizzy who was smiling back at her. "When your aunt gets an idea in her head, there's no stopping her. I'd say we can be pretty sure that the end-of-summer show is going to be the best ever. Now go help me saddle up Summer and Scout. You can give Lindsay and I some pointers."

"You're going to need them," Tizzy teased back.

*****

The shadows danced across the path and made Cole think of the game she used to play when she was a kid, trying to guess what shape the clouds looked like. If she tried real hard, she could do the same things with the shadows now as they lay across the gravel path she was walking. With her mind wandering, Cole didn't even hear Danny as he jogged up behind her.

"Hey, Cole." He stopped beside her, breathing hard from his run. "Didn't think I would see anyone on this path."

Cole turned, a little bit startled. "Oh, hi, Danny, I'm just out for a walk." Cole was surprised at how happy she was to see him.

"You seemed to be thinking pretty hard when I ran up. Anything on your mind?"

"No, not really." Cole laughed at herself. "I was just playing a silly little game." Danny tilted his head, interested in what she had to say. "I was trying to make shapes out of the shadows of the trees and flowers, like how you can do with the clouds. Then I got to thinking how it's funny, you know? Shadows can be so scary at night, but in the day, you can see them for what they really are. They're really nothing to be afraid of."

Danny liked Cole. He liked the way she thought. He hadn't spent much time with her yet, but he hoped he would have the chance to change that in the future. So far, all the time he had spent with her had made him realize how unique she was. She was always thinking, always trying to understand life and her place in it. Danny never took anything quite so seriously, and he found her thoughtfulness refreshing.

"You're right, I guess. I think that's like a lot of things. How you go through times when something can seem scary or hard to understand. Then, out of the blue, a light can shine, and you can see that what you were scared of is nothing to be afraid of. You can see it for what it is and accept it." Cole and Danny walked along at a slow pace, in no hurry to finish their walk.

"That's how I feel with Tizzy. With this whole camp," Cole confessed, "that's what I was really thinking about."

Danny turned to look at her and could see the stress and worry etched on her forehead. "What do you mean?"

"I'm just waiting for the light to shine."

"It will come. It always does. You just have to be patient."

*****

Ashton,

I so wish you could come back early! We're doing this Adventure Triathlon event next week (Lindsay says it will be great publicity for the camp), and I wish you could compete with me! It's a competition we're having with the camps next door. Well, we haven't asked ERA yet, but Still Waters is in. Cole and Lindsay have been working so hard to set it all up. The race is three events. First you have to sail a short course, then mountain bike, and then finish with a horse-riding event. The girls from our camp have been practicing on the dinghies a little bit, and Cole and Tizzy have been giving riding lessons to the boys next door who are going to compete. I can't wait.

Things seem to be really turning around here. I'm sure it's not a surprise to you, but I'm surprised. I would never have imagined my aunts and me getting along this well. They're so different from my parents and from me and from each other, really. Ha! But it's nice. Now that we've spent almost the whole summer together (can you believe it's been over two months?) I feel like I finally know them. Sometimes there are even moments when I see one of them move or talk a certain way, and it reminds me so much of my mom. Like Lindsay's laugh. She laughs at her own jokes. I mean really, Ashton, she cracks herself up all the time. But her laugh is just like my mom's. Sometimes it makes me miss my mom even more, but sometimes, I'm just happy to catch a glimpse of her again. I don't know if that makes any sense.

Anyways, I hope you've gotten to do some riding in Quebec. Danielle, the girl from next door whom I'm helping to train on Peaches, is actually getting pretty good. I think it might be a miracle, ha!

Can't wait for you to come home!

Au revoir!

Tizzy

*****

"Can you believe it, Tizzy? Sheila actually laughed when Callie fell off. It was horrible. This is Callie's first year at camp, so she's really just a beginner, and she was doing awesome. She's already started jumping and was going over two foot fences when her horse just balked. She literally flew over his head." Thankfully Peaches was standing still, Danielle was talking with her hands so much Tizzy was sure she would have yanked the bit right out of the horse's mouth. "It was horrible. Sheila, a few of the other girls and I were lined up on the fence watching and Sheila started giggling. I can't stand her." Danielle practically growled.

"She sounds horrible," Tizzy agreed. "I'm glad I don't have to deal with her."

"Trust me, you're lucky." Danielle nudged Peaches forward, and they took off around the barrels at a lope. *She lookes great,* Tizzy thought. There had been a few days where she wondered if Danielle was going to be a lost cause, but then, one day, it just seemed to click. All of a sudden, she looked like a natural, like she should be wearing cowboy boots instead of black knee-high jumping boots.

"Nice! Now lean in!" Tizzy shouted as Peaches round the third barrel. "Give him full rein!" Danielle leaned forward coming out of the last barrel and did as Tizzy said, giving the horse her full head so she could stretch into the gallop as they raced back to the finish line.

Tizzy hit the stop watch as they crossed between the cones. "You clocked a 23.8! That's amazing, Danielle!"

Danielle let out a whoop that pierced the air and did a victory lap, Peaches' gold mane flying in the wind. Tizzy laughed. This was what she loved about riding—the competition and accomplishments in barrel racing. Then when it was all done, the realization that you didn't do it by yourself. You have your horse to thank for the other half.

Chapter *15*

The gate at the entrance of the European Riding Academy was enormous and made of wrought iron. It had sharp edges and stood out against the light-blue sky. The camp's name ran across the top, and then below it, the camp's motto was etched in steel, "Where winners are bred."

"Whoa," Cole whispered, "I don't think I can do this."

"Yes, you can. We're doing this together," Lindsay replied as she and Cole both stood outside the gate, staring up at the camp motto. "And besides, you know I'll do most of the talking." Lindsay reached over to the intercom that was stationed outside the gate and hit the button.

"European Riding Academy, how can I help you?" The voice sounded tinny through the little box.

"Yes, hi, this is Lindsay and Cole Burns from next door. We run Green Hills Adventure Camp. We're really hoping to talk to Alberta Highland." Lindsay paused, "Please."

"Hold one minute please."

"I can't believe they're making us stand outside and wait," Lindsay vented, irritated at their neighbor's rudeness. Static broke through the intercom, "She says she has five minutes." The gate buzzed and slowly began to open. Cole and Lindsay looked at each other and then walked through.

*****

They hadn't been inside these gates in ten years. Back when they were kids it had been a riding camp, but the owners were friends with their parents, and there was never any competition. When they sold the camp and Alberta Highland had purchased the prime real estate, apparently everything had changed. They had heard bits and pieces of the story from Ann, but just like Ann would, she never made their relationship with the neighbors sound as bad as it was.

"Can you believe it? This is serious money." Lindsay leaned in to Cole and tilted her head over toward the barn and girls' dormitory. Both were made of gray brick with white shutters and doors. The dormitory had ivy growing up the side. The barn was large with individual turnouts attached to each stall. The two women headed straight toward the main building and passed groups of girls wearing their riding camp's mandatory uniforms on their way.

"Can you imagine sending Tizzy here?" Cole asked.

"No, are you kidding me? It would be like tossing her to the wolves," Lindsay joked. "These girls look like they're seventeen."

"She could hold her own," Cole defended, "but it doesn't mean I would want to send her here. It's so serious, so harsh looking." *Even if it is beautiful,* she thought. Apparently, money could buy you nice buildings and beautiful horses, but it didn't seem to be buying any of the girls they saw a lot of fun. "I hope that the Evergreen Boarding School isn't anything like this."

"We'll have to go look at it." Lindsay started up the stone stairs to the front entrance, "*If* that's what we decide to do." Cole caught the uncertainty in Lindsay's voice at the idea of sending Tizzy away and knew that it matched her own feelings toward their original idea for the end of summer.

"We're here to speak with Alberta," Lindsay said to the secretary.

"Headmistress Highland will be right out."

"Sheesh, they don't expect us to call her that, do they?" Cole muttered under her breath as she and Lindsay took a seat in the straight high-backed chairs in the reception room. Fifteen minutes later, they were ushered into a large dark-paneled room with very little furniture. The only décor on the walls was an oil painting of an English fox hunt that hung behind the oak desk where Alberta Highland was seated.

"What can I do for you, ladies?" she quipped, not even inviting the sisters to sit down.

"We've tried to call you," Cole noticed a hard edge to Lindsay's voice that she rarely heard and knew from the start that this wasn't going to go well, "several times in fact, but unfortunately, we were never allowed through to your line. You must be very busy, so we won't take too much of your time." Alberta's head tilted as she sensed the challenging tone in Lindsay's voice. It was not a tone she was used to hearing coming from others. "We, being the good people that we are," Cole had to stifle a giggle at Lindsay's serious tone, "just wanted to do the neighborly thing and invite you and your campers to participate in an adventure triathlon that we are hosting at Green Hills. Still Waters has already accepted. I have a flyer here advertising the event that we have sent out to the community and to our campers' parents." Lindsay set the beautifully presented flyer that she had worked so hard on creating on the large desk. Alberta's eyes didn't even flinch downward to look nor did she reach for the paper.

"Thank you," she said without any sincerity, "but, no. We here at ERA do not participate in adventure triathlons or whatever you are calling this thing. We are a riding academy. My students are here to learn from the best trainers, on the best horses, how to be the best competitive riders. We don't have time for BBQs and barrel racing." Alberta had finally looked down at the advertisement and noticed that there was a community BBQ to be held after the event.

Cole stood in silence, shaking at the severity of Alberta's cold gray eyes. "That's great." Lindsay smiled and took a step toward the headmistress. "That is just what we were hoping you would say." She grabbed Cole's hand and stormed out of the room, not bothering to close the door behind her.

*****

Behind the immense gray building and underneath the open window crouched Danielle, Callie, and two other newcomers to ERA. When they heard Cole and Lindsay leave the office, they crawled away and didn't say a word until they were far enough from the window to not be overheard. "I can't believe she said no!" Callie cried.

"I can," Danielle muttered back, "it would have been too good to be true." Tizzy had told Danielle about the Adventure Triathlon at one of their early morning lessons and when Danielle saw Tizzy's aunts walking to the main office, she had a feeling that they were here to talk about it. She and her friends had rushed around to the back of the building to listen in on the conversation.

"This totally sucks. It would have been so good to get out of here just for a day, and I've been dying to see what the other camps are like," a small girl with red hair said and sighed.

Danielle hadn't told anyone about her riding lessons over at Green Hills. All the other girls just thought she went off to read during the morning free session. Most everybody else spent that time all spread out either gossiping in the dorm rooms or working in the art studios, so Danielle was never really missed. "This isn't right." Danielle jutted out her chin. "Every other camp on this island is participating. We should be allowed to do it too." With that, she turned on her heel and strode quickly toward the front of the building.

"Danielle, wait!" Callie called. "Oh great, now we're in for it," she whispered to the other girls as they ran after her. When they reached the long drive-way that lead from the entrance gate to the main building, they stopped short. In a straight path from the exit of the main building, as far as she could see was a trail of brightly colored flyers. Danielle reached down to pick one up. It was on thick glossy paper with color photos of a rider she recognized as Tizzy, racing around barrels. It also had a photo of boys in a sailboat with Still Waters written in cursive on the side of the dinghy.

Orcas Island's First Annual Adventure Triathlon
Saturday, August 24
hosted by Green Hills Adventure Camp

Danielle read the rest of the flyer that described what would be the most fun day of summer on Orcas Island. She looked down the drive and saw that other campers were picking up the flyers and reading them, showing them to each other. *Headmistress Highland would have to change her mind now,* she thought and laughed.

*****

"I can't believe you did that!" Cole nearly shrieked as they walked home. Lindsay tugged her oversize purse that had held all the flyers up higher on her shoulder.

"Did what?" She smirked at her sister and kept on walking.

"Come on, Lindsay, she is going to be *so* mad at us."

"I'll just tell her they fell out of my purse. She threw us out of there so fast I didn't want to slow down to pick them up." At that, Cole couldn't help herself and started laughing. Lindsay joined in too until the two of them had tears running down their cheeks. The whole way home, the sun shone down on the two sisters who, for all the world to see, couldn't seem happier.

Chapter *16*

"She said no! Can you believe it?" Danielle was hysterical the next day at her riding lesson with Tizzy. "Your aunts are geniuses with that stunt they pulled, and she still said no." Tizzy wasn't quite sure what to say to Danielle. She was so worked up. "You should have heard the whole camp, most of them anyways. Sheila and her crew were saying they wouldn't want to do it anyways, but everyone else thought they were crazy, so they were just sitting in the corner pouting like babies. It was great. The rest of us still can't believe she said no. You should have heard her, Tizzy. She came over the intercom system with her deep booming voice and called a whole camp meeting in the cafeteria. We all had to go wait for her to show up to tell us that,

'In no uncertain terms would anyone from ERA be participating in any sort of adventure games.' Can you believe it? People started talking and arguing so loud that when she couldn't quiet us down she just stormed off the stage and left."

Tizzy's aunts hadn't told her what they had done with the flyers. They had just come home and said that ERA had chosen not to participate. Which was fine with her and her aunts too, it seemed. She wasn't even sure why her aunts had invited the European Riding Academy, but it seemed like something that they would do just because they thought they should.

"I am never going back there, not for another summer. I don't care what my parents say," Danielle nearly yelled, causing Peaches to flick her ears back and dance away from her on the lead rope.

Now, Tizzy realized, maybe there was another benefit to her aunts showing all the campers next door the fun things they did at Green Hills. Hopefully, she thought, Danielle would be the first of many new campers next year at Green Hills.

*****

She knew it! Sheila almost couldn't keep quiet as she hid behind some shrubs and pulled out her cell phone. Sheila had known from the start that something was up with Danielle. She couldn't stand the girl. Danielle had even gone so far as to tell Amy Mansfield that Sheila had talked about her behind her back. Now Amy was spending more time with

Danielle, and that was ruining her whole plan. She had figured that if she got close enough with Amy at camp this summer, then she would get to hang out more at her house during the school year, which meant she would see more of Beau. He was a year older than them, so she didn't get to see him very much in school, but she was sure he liked her. *All the boys do*, she thought. Anger boiled up in her as she opened up the camera app and lifted the lens to get a clear shot of Danielle sneaking under the fence wire into the barnyard of the camp next door. *A barnyard,* she thought with disgust, *this place looks horrible. Who would ever want to go there?* She took several pictures, and then when she was sure she had enough proof to show Headmistress Highland, she quickly turned around and ran back to camp.

*****

"Where's Cole?" Tizzy asked Lindsay at breakfast the next morning.

"Oh she's in town at the art gallery. Carol, the lady who owns it, was a good friend of your moms. She's agreed to try selling some of Cole's pottery."

"That's great." Tizzy smiled. She knew that Cole had been working on converting the shed behind the main house into an art studio and had even had Danny help her install a kiln she had bought second hand from someone in Seattle.

"You're back early this morning. Is Danielle so good she doesn't need lessons anymore?" Lindsay teased.

"No, well, she is getting pretty good actually"—Tizzy frowned—"but today, she didn't show up."

"Really? Maybe she's not feeling well."

"I don't know, maybe." Tizzy got up to pour herself a bowl of cereal. She hoped it was that simple, but for some reason, she thought it might be more.

*****

Lindsay was sitting at her desk in a small corner of the living room working on a project. "I'm going to have to do something about this office situation," she muttered to herself. She had been picking up a few freelance marketing jobs this summer, and over the last few weeks, her business had really grown. She was good at what she did, she knew that, but she didn't know she would have so much freelance work. She felt confident that if the pace kept up like this, she could make a living outside of New York. *Maybe even on this island,* she thought then pushed the thought away. Lindsay felt guilty just thinking about the end of the summer. She was pretty sure she and Cole were on the same page with how they felt about the camp and about Tizzy, but she couldn't commit quite yet. She didn't want to say anything to Cole either. If she said it out loud, it would seem real, and then she would feel committed, and she wasn't ready to take that step. This wasn't ever what she thought her life would look like, and Lindsay had a hard time changing directions and straying from her plan. Being focused was what had gotten her so far in life, hadn't it? Why should she have to change the way she was? But then, she imagined what she would lose if she left the island and felt confused all over again.

Her thoughts were interrupted by a pounding on the door. "Tizzy, can you get that?" After a few seconds and no response, Lindsay figured that Tizzy had gone back to the barn. She got up to answer the door. The face that was glaring back at her was pure fury. Alberta Highland stood straight as an arrow, shoulders pulled back, and a sneer on her face. Her upper lip quivered with anger. *She looks like she's going to spit,* Lindsay thought, and was ready to step back quickly if she needed to.

"There *isn't a gate,* so I just let myself in." She looked down her nose at Lindsay who was almost a foot shorter than her.

Lindsay rose discreetly up onto her toes. "How can I help you?" she said, her voice as sweet as honey.

"If you *ever* try to steal my campers again"—her face clouded like a storm passed over it—"I will close your small camp down in the blink of an eye."

"I'm not sure what you're talking about," Lindsay's voice deepened, and she stepped toward Alberta.

"This." She held up a cell phone with a blurry picture of Danielle coming onto Green Hills property. "And this!" Alberta thrust a handful of

Lindsay's flyers back at her. They were crumpled and torn in half.

"Oh, I'm sure this is all a misunderstanding. I dropped these on my way out of your camp yesterday. Thank you for returning them. And this"—she nodded toward the cell phone—"I'm sure you remember me calling you earlier this summer. I was calling to clear this with you. I knew that Danielle was coming over here, but since you weren't concerned enough to talk about it with me, I assumed you were okay with it."

"Well, I'm not!" Alberta snapped.

"Fine by me. There's only a week left of camp anyways." She started to shut the door. "Oh, by the way, Tizzy just told me this morning that your young camper has become quite the barrel racer. We only breed the best over here too." Lindsay smiled and slammed the door.

*****

"Oh great, Lindsay." Worry lines crossed Cole's forehead. "Can we get in trouble for this?"

"Of course not." The two sisters sat on the brown leather sofa in the living room while Lindsay recounted the visit with Alberta. Lindsay got up and walked to the desk in the corner and pulled out a file folder. She came back to the couch and curled her knees up under her.

"I don't know how you can be so calm about this. What if she talks to Danielle's parents?" Cole asked.

Lindsay lifted a single piece of paper out of the file and held it out to Cole. "*I* already did." A wide smile spread across Lindsay's face. "I called them up weeks ago. After Alberta refused to give us the time of day when we first tried to talk to her, I told Danielle that she couldn't continue the lessons without me first talking to her parents. She was all worried that they wouldn't let her, but she finally gave in and gave me their number when she realized I was serious about not letting her ride here anymore." Cole looked at Lindsay in amazement. "I called and talked to her dad. Once I mentioned that we were willing to give Danielle *free riding lessons* if they would sign a waiver, he couldn't have agreed fast enough. He told me that Danielle's mom and him were spending enough money on fancy camps and riding lessons that he would take anything he could get for free. I e-mailed him the waiver, which he signed and faxed over that day."

"You're a genius." Cole laughed and hugged her sister.

"I just e-mailed Alberta a copy of the signed waiver right before you got here. I don't think Danielle's parents will want to hear that the camp headmistress has no idea what her campers are doing throughout the day. I doubt she'll contact them to say anything once she realizes they knew more about Danielle's daily activities than she did."

Cole couldn't believe it. Her sister had been five steps ahead the whole time. She smiled when she realized she actually wasn't even surprised.

Chapter 17

"Still Waters is completely taking care of the sailing portion of the triathlon, so we just have to handle the mountain biking and barrel racing parts. Now that we know ERA isn't participating, we decided that the last leg of the race would be a timed barrel racing run," Tizzy explained to Ruthie as they sat on wood deck chairs and looked out over the water. Cole and Lindsay had gone next door for a planning session with Danny, so Ruthie had made oatmeal chocolate chip cookies for her and Tizzy to enjoy on the deck for dessert. "Of course, Lindsay made an enormous list." Tizzy rolled her blue eyes. "She has it scheduled out for everything we need to get done over the next five days, morning until night. She even scheduled lunch breaks."

Ruthie laughed out loud. "That sounds like your aunt. I'm sure you guys will get everything done if you follow her list."

"Lindsay says we have to turn the place into a 'first-rate facility' if we ever hope of competing with the other camps. She has us cleaning parts of the camp that the guests won't even see." Tizzy frowned at the idea of all the work. "I'm scheduled to clean the bathrooms on Thursday at 4:00. See?" She held out the schedule she pulled from her jean pocket. Ruthie took the list and looked it over. "Lindsay says we can't overestimate the importance of a first impression on all these potential clients."

"Campers," Ruthie corrected, "your aunt may see this place as a business, but I want you to remember it's a camp first." Ruthie offered Tizzy the plate of cookies, and she grabbed two more. "Really, that's what's great about your aunts. The camp can't run unless it makes money, but someone has to also see to the heart of the place. Do you know what I mean, Tizzy? They balance each other out."

"Yeah, I guess they do," Tizzy paused, wondering if she should voice what she had been hoping for all along. "That's why they're perfect."

"Perfect for what, hon?"

"To run the camp. To make it first rate again. They wouldn't be putting in all this work if they weren't going to keep it open, right? Lindsay hates getting dirty. They wouldn't do all this if they were just going to leave." Tizzy sounded so hopeful it nearly broke Ruthie's heart.

"I don't know, Tiz. They haven't said anything to me. What I do know is that both your aunts had full lives before this summer. They might not be able to leave those lives, no matter how much they might want to." Ruthie could see Tizzy's confidence fading. "I know they love you, hon. I do too. No matter what happens at the end of summer, we will always love you."

"I know that. I love you too. But there is *no way* they are going to do all this work for nothing."

Unless they're fixing it up to sell it, Ruthie thought but couldn't bring herself to say it to the girl. Ruthie didn't know what the future held, but if Tizzy could have hope, then she would have hope too. The alternative was too crushing to face.

"They're planning on staying. I'm sure of it." The smile returned to Tizzy's face, and she leaned in and hugged Ruthie gently. Ruthie always smelled like cinnamon and mint. To Tizzy, she smelled like home.

*****

"You girls are going to work yourselves to death," Ruthie scolded as she walked back onto the mountain biking course where Cole, Lindsay, and Tizzy were setting up directional flags and digging holes for post markers. "You could at least stop for a drink." The three girls turned as Ruthie approached them, holding a glass pitcher of her famous mint iced tea. Ruthie had been making the same iced tea recipe since they were young girls.

"That looks great!" Cole said as she helped Ruthie set the glasses and pitcher on a nearby log, and the others joined them, sitting on various stumps.

Ruthie smiled at the three girls. "What are you girls doing out here in the dirt for goodness sake?"

"Redirecting the bike route." Tizzy smiled from ear to ear. "Trying to make it a little bit easier for the beginners."

"I don't know why all that work makes you so happy?" Ruthie teased, but remembering her conversation with Tizzy last night, Ruthie knew exactly why Tizzy was smiling like that. Here they were, putting in hard work, and in Tizzy's mind, that meant that her aunts were staying and so was she.

"Hey guys! We just finished setting up the buoys for the sailing course, so we figured we'd head over here and see if you needed any help." Danny led a string of eight boys following in step behind him.

"Many hands make light work," Cole called out and wiped the sweat from her forehead. "Thanks guys, we've still got quite a bit of work left here." She jogged up to Danny and gave him a quick hug.

"We'll even share our tea with you," Lindsay winked at all the newcomers.

"I'll go get some more glasses," Ruthie added and took off toward the house.

Lindsay started giving out directions, sending the boys all over the mountain biking course to set up flags and cones, dig deeper trenches along the sides of the path, and to start assembling the bleachers they had brought in for the spectators.

"Hey, Tizzy." Beau walked up to her and grabbed the shovel Cole had set down. "Can you believe it's almost here?"

Tizzy looked at Beau, his sun-tanned face seemed to shine, and for the first time, she noticed all of his freckles and not his scar. She felt like they had been friends for a long time. "No, this summer flew by. Are you ready for the race?"

"Yeah, but I'm not sure how I'm going to do barrel racing." He laughed. "It's been fun practicing, though. I didn't think I would like it so much. It just goes to show you never really know."

Tizzy smiled. *How could anyone not like riding?* she thought, then reasoned that she hadn't been too sure about the sailing part of the competition and surprised herself with how much fun she was having over at Still Waters practicing.

Tizzy and Beau continued to work, their conversation flowing smoothly and without pause. Other campers joined them, asking Tizzy for tips on barrel racing. Cole and Lindsay stopped to watch their niece hard at work with the other kids.

"She looks happy, doesn't she?" Cole asked.

"Yeah," Lindsay watched Tizzy closely. The young girl was laughing with the others and talking animatedly. "She does. It's amazing really. She's been through so much this year."

"She's a strong girl," Cole answered, and both sisters stood, stretching their aching backs and looking on at the girl they had come to love.

Chapter 18

Tizzy stood with her cowboy boots up on the bottom rung of the fence surrounding the riding arena and leaned her elbows over the top railing. "That's it, Cole. Don't lock your knees!" she shouted at her aunt who was in the ring standing on Summer's back while she galloped around the outer edge of the arena. Cole spread her arms out and kept her balance, totally in tune with the rhythm of the horse's gait.

"Since when did you learn so much about trick riding?" Lindsay asked as she leaned against the fence next to Tizzy, keeping a steady eye on Cole.

"Since you guys said you were doing a show and I've been watching nonstop YouTube videos." Tizzy smiled as her aunt playfully bumped her with her shoulder.

"Should we start calling you coach?"

"Sounds good to me. You're up next." Tizzy and Lindsay watched as Cole gracefully crouched down and swung herself back into the saddle. She pulled Summer up next to the girls on the fence and pushed her hat back, breathing hard.

"I forgot how much work this is. You're up, little sis." She dismounted and handed the reins to Lindsay. "Why don't you warm up and I'll go saddle up Scout. Then we can go through the routine together. Tizzy can play the music."

"Sure, sounds good. Give me some pointers, Tiz," Lindsay winked at her niece. "Lord knows I could use some." She turned and mounted Summer before trotting off. Tizzy loved watching her aunts. They were in perfect harmony with their horses. She couldn't believe they could pick up riding again so fast, even the difficult tricks. Cole said it was like riding a bike though. You never really forget how to do it, especially when your growing up years revolve around horses. Tizzy could sense that her aunts had missed riding, though. They had been spending hours practicing for this show, and all the time they weren't weeding the garden or cleaning the bunkhouses, they were on Summer and Scout's back. As far as Tizzy could see, they were their happiest when they were riding.

Tizzy's mind was snapped back into reality when Cole came riding out on Scout.

"All right, Tiz," Cole shouted, "press play on the stereo, and then it's time for you to go inside for a while. Lindsay and I have to practice our last trick, and we want to keep it a secret."

"A secret? Why?"

"Because we want you to watch our show and be amazed at how incredible we are," Lindsay teased. "You're not going to think we're awesome if you've seen the whole performance a hundred times."

"All right, all right." Tizzy climbed off the railing and started sulking back toward the house. She walked slowly, thinking about what her aunt had said and knew that she was right. Sometimes, when you see something or someone a lot, you start to take it for granted. Pip ran up alongside of her and Tizzy reached down to pat her head. "You can't get too comfortable with what you see and always expect it to be there," she whispered to the dog. Looking back now, she realized she had done that with her parents, even with the camp. It was what she saw every day, so she expected it would last forever. Tizzy opened the front door of her house and looked back, but the barn was out of sight. She wouldn't do that with her aunts. She reminded herself of her earlier promise not to take her aunts for granted.

*****

When the sun rose on Friday morning Lindsay was already down in the kitchen sipping boiling hot coffee out of her favorite mug. She had her laptop out on the kitchen table and was rechecking her to-do list to make sure everything had been completed. She was so engrossed in her work she didn't hear Tizzy come down the stairs at 7:30.

"You're up early," Tizzy commented.

"Geez, Tizzy!" Lindsay startled, nearly jumping out of her chair.

"Sorry I didn't mean to scare you." Tizzy laughed.

"It's okay. I just woke up early this morning, lots of last-minute things to check on." The truth was, Lindsay had barely slept. A lot rode on this once simple triathlon that had turned into an end-of-summer celebration, island gathering, and multi-camp party. Lindsay was afraid they had bit off more than they could chew, and now it was too late to go back.

"Well, I'm yours all day. I don't have anything to do but finish setting up, and we've already done most of that."

"Thanks, Tizzy. You've been such a big help."

Tizzy got up. "I'm going to go shower before breakfast, and then we can start on the last items on your checklist." Tizzy turned and ran up the stairs, passing Cole on her way down.

"Morning, Tizzy." Cole smiled as the girl soared past her. "She's in a hurry this morning."

"Yeah, I think she's excited to finally get everything finished. It's been a long week with a lot of work," Lindsay replied. Cole noticed that Lindsay looked exhausted. She felt the same way.

"Everything has come together though, don't you think?"

"Yeah, it has. We just won't know if all of this work has paid off until we see if anyone signs up for camp next summer. We're taking a big gamble, Cole, leaving our jobs and our homes behind. It just makes me nervous. Running a small business, especially a summer camp, is risky." Lindsay sighed and laid her head down on her folded hands on the table.

"We'll figure it out as we go, Lindsay. That's one thing we've all had to learn this summer. Nothing is for sure."

Lindsay raised her head and looked up at her sister. "How are you always so calm?" Lindsay whined.

"I'm not." Cole tilted her head and smiled. "I'm just faking it." Both girls burst into laughter. "Here"—Cole went for the oatmeal—"let's eat. We've got a big day ahead of us."

The two sisters sat together and went over the finishing touches they would need to work on today. There were still quite a few things around the camp that needed their attention. Tizzy was just about to come back downstairs when her aunt's conversation floated toward her and caught her attention. She came to a quiet stop on the upstairs landing.

"We'll need to call Evergreen Boarding Academy first thing on Monday morning," Cole reminded Lindsay.

"Okay, I'll take care of that. All the other arrangements can be taken care of next week. We'll need to book flights to New York and Nevada as soon as possible too."

"So that's it. We've decided?"

"Yep. Not everyone will be happy about it, but we're doing what's best."

Only a few yards away, Tizzy couldn't breathe. She couldn't believe what she was hearing. She had been so sure, so thankful, that her aunts would stay on Orcas Island with her and they would keep the camp, her last connection to her parents. *What a joke that had been,* she thought. She hated them. She. Hated. Them. They didn't care about her at all. They didn't love her. It had all been lies and make-believe. Without a sound, Tizzy turned around and crept back into the bathroom.

*****

She couldn't face them. Tizzy didn't think that she would be able to hide the fact that she knew they were getting rid of her, sending her off to some sort of boarding school. Obviously, they were trying to keep it a secret, and this was a game she didn't want to play. Tizzy felt like the air was being sucked out of her. She leaned back against the tiled wall and wept. She had to get out. She had to leave, and she had to do it now. Tizzy grabbed the bathroom window and leaned into it, trying to make it budge. This was one of the things on Lindsay's endless list. The windows in this house always stuck. She got her shoulder under it and shoved harder. It came open in one quick motion, and Tizzy almost flew out the window. Looking down, Tizzy felt no fear, only adrenaline and a need to escape. She hoisted herself out the window feet first, onto the trellis her father had built just two years ago. Her mom had planted clematis on the trellis, but it hadn't quite taken over yet and left her plenty of spots to place her feet. Her feet hit the dry dirt in a thud as she dropped the last few feet.

"Now what?" she muttered to herself. She wiped the tears streaking her face with the back of her hand. Looking up, she saw the waters of the Puget Sound and, without much thought, took off running to the beach. Hopefully, Lindsay and Cole wouldn't see her as she sprinted across the lawn toward the path leading down to the water.

*****

"What's wrong, Pip?" Cole cooed at the small, whimpering dog. Pip sat at the base of the stairs and pawed the ground.

"Come here, girl," Lindsay called, but Pip wouldn't move. "She must sense all of the excitement around here." Lindsay stood and stretched her arms above her head. "Okay, we've got a lot to do. I'm going to go get dressed, then we can meet out at the barn in half an hour."

"Sounds good." Cole smiled at her sister and then looked back at the dog, her back was to the kitchen window as Tizzy ran across the lawn.

Chapter 19

Tizzy stared out over the water, the waves rolling in peacefully and the air already balmy. It was supposed to be a beautiful weekend, something Lindsay had been praying for, hoping the Seattle rain wouldn't dump on the heads of the spectators. *Our potential clients. All lies,* Tizzy thought. Her heart felt like it was breaking, and it shocked her. She didn't think her heart had ever healed since her parent's deaths, and now, the realization that it could break even further hit her like a punch in the gut. She didn't know what to do. Her eyes scanned the water and landed on Still Waters' beach. It was quiet there, the campers probably still getting up and eating breakfast in the mess hall. Tizzy's eyes caught sight of the sailboats set up for the race tomorrow.

They were all tethered to the dock, swaying gently in the current. Tizzy sat up straight. Everything she had thought was about to happen in her life had just shattered, and all she knew was that she didn't want to be here. She wanted to be with her parents.

The decision was made before she even knew it. She was up and running toward the neighboring dock, eyeing the small white sailboat at the edge that would be the easiest for her to navigate alone out onto the open water. Tizzy heard Pip barking shrilly as she chased Tizzy down the beach and out onto the dock. At the last minute, as Tizzy was untying the dinghy, Pip jumped in, and Tizzy let her stay.

*****

"Where's Tiz? I thought she'd be the first one out here," Lindsay wondered and looked around the barnyard.

"I didn't see her upstairs. She must've slipped down when we were getting ready. I'm sure she'll be out soon." Cole and Lindsay headed toward the tack room where they kept all their grooming supplies. They planned on grooming every single horse today and braiding their manes until they sparkled and shined. It was going to be a long, hot afternoon.

*****

Tizzy and Pip crossed the water quicker and smoother than she had expected. "I probably would have done well tomorrow on the sailing course," Tizzy said sadly to her dog. Tizzy had sailed right up onto the sandbar, just as she had seen Beau do the last time they sailed out to Horseshoe Island. It had been less than an hour since she had overheard her aunt's conversation, and in that short time, her whole life, her whole future, had changed. Tizzy took off her tennis shoes and jumped with Pip out into the cold gray water and up onto the sandy beach. The sand felt warm between her toes and Tizzy plopped down on the soft ground.

"I don't know what to do, Pip." Tizzy rested her hand on the soft red fur of her best friend. "At least you seem to want me. No one else does." Then the tears started all over again.

*****

"Cole! Lindsay!" Ruthie came running out to the barn, a dishtowel thrown over her shoulder, and her hair falling out of its usual bun. She was out of breath by the time the girls heard her and came over to the fence at a jog.

"What's wrong?" Cole asked.

"Danny's been calling your cell phone non-stop. I was in the kitchen baking for tomorrow, and I finally answered it for you. He says there's some sort of emergency. Something about a boat. I said you would call him back as soon as I found you guys."

Lindsay and Cole sprinted back to the house, curious about what was going on next door. Cole ran straight into the kitchen where she had left her cell phone and dialed Danny's number.

"Danny, what's the emergency?" Cole rushed out as soon as Danny answered the phone.

"One of the boats is missing." There was something in Danny's tone that made Cole nervous. "I'm not sure what's happened, but I know it didn't just come loose. I secured the boats myself last night."

"That's horrible." Cole immediately thought of the cost of a boat and all the damage that could come to it. Danny's job could be on the line if something happened to the camp property under his watch. "What could've happened?"

"I'm not exactly sure. Something just doesn't feel right. I lined the boats up last night for the competition tomorrow then secured them all." Lindsay leaned in to Cole's cell phone so she could hear the conversation. "I'm going to talk to all the campers. Can you ask around there and see if anyone noticed anything or saw anyone?"

"Yeah, sure. I'm sure it'll turn up. It'll be okay," Cole tried to reassure Danny, but she wasn't sure she believed it herself. Once she hung up, she relayed the conversation to Ruthie and Lindsay, but no one had been down to the beach today or seen anything.

"Let's ask Tiz," Lindsay said. "Ruthie, have you seen her? She wasn't out at the barn with us."

"No, I haven't seen her all day. I thought she left with you guys."

"She's probably out in the barn now. I'll go check. One of you guys look out over the bluff on the beach and the other check the biking course. She's got to be in one of those places." Lindsay handed out the orders but had a nagging feeling in her gut that something wasn't quite right.

Chapter 20

The three ladies searched the grounds of the camp, calling out Tizzy's name for fifteen minutes before they met back up at the main house. They each knew she was gone. It was more of a feeling than anything; the place felt empty without Tizzy.

Cole reached for her cell and called Danny back, "Danny, Tizzy's not here. We can't find her, and Pip's gone too. That dog never leaves her side."

"I had a feeling," Danny answered quietly, as if he wished he didn't have to tell her what he knew. "I looked more closely down at the dock. There are tracks in the sand coming from the direction of your camp. Two actually, if you count the dogs."

"Danny! Where did she go? She doesn't know what she's doing out there." Cole began to cry, and Lindsay put her arm around her.

"She'll be okay, Cole, she's actually pretty good. I've seen her handle a boat when we've been practicing. We just need to find her." His voice was calm, and he hoped it didn't betray the nerves he felt. "Meet me down at the dock. I'll sail out and see if I can find her." Cole hung up and raced out the door, Lindsay and Ruthie not far behind.

*****

"Danny!" Beau called out as he chased after him.

Danny only barely slowed, still heading toward the beach. "What is it, bud?"

"I know I shouldn't have been listening, but I heard you on the deck talking to Tizzy's aunt." Beau looked down at his shoes, embarrassed about having eavesdropped. Danny waited patiently for the boy to continue. "It's just, if Tizzy went sailing, I think I know where she might have gone."

Danny's eyes snapped to attention. "Where, Beau?" His voice was calm but serious.

"Tizzy told me about this island, she calls it Horseshoe Island. It was somewhere she always went with her parents. We sailed out there that one day, remember? It's the island just north of here. Anytime I've seen her practicing on the boat the last few weeks, she's always heading in that direction. I'm not sure she's ever actually sailed that far by herself, though."

Danny put his hand on Beau's shoulder. The boy looked nervous, unsure if he should have said anything at all. "Thanks, Beau, you did the right thing." Danny turned back toward the water and took off at a run. It was already after lunch, and he wasn't sure how long the boat had been gone. He knew it was a risk to follow Beau's instinct. There were fewer islands to the north, leaving Tizzy less options, and Danny thought it was a more natural and easier course to head south, but Danny had watched Beau all summer. He was a kind kid, observant, and aware of other people's feelings. He felt that Beau knew what he was talking about.

*****

Tizzy didn't know how long she had been lying in the sand. A long time she guessed, as her stomach growled with hunger. The tears on her cheeks had dried, and she felt exhausted. Tizzy could see the camp from where she lay, but she knew they couldn't see her boat. She had beached it at the eastern tip of the horseshoe where it would be out of sight. She hadn't wanted to be found right away. Actually, she realized, she didn't want to be found at all. But as she lay there, she came to understand that she had nowhere to go, no home, no family, no one who loved her the way her parents had. Tizzy squinted her eyes until she could see the tiny speck that was Green Hills Adventure camp. Oddly enough, even though she guessed it was midday by the fact that the sun was directly overhead, the porch light seemed to be on at the main house. Lindsay had just changed all the camp lights last week to LED lights. She said they were brighter and more efficient. Why had they been working so hard on the camp and putting effort into it if they were just going to leave, she wondered. Maybe they're just fixing it up to sell. Ruthie had said that was a possibility. Now she felt foolish for not listening. Tizzy stared at that porch light for so long her head started to ache. *It's as bright as a star,* she thought, and remembered lying on the lawn with her aunts just a few weeks ago talking about the stars, about how the North Star always led her mom home, back to the camp where she belonged.

In that moment, Tizzy knew. She knew that Green Hills was her home, the place where she fit, where she belonged. Even if her aunts sent her to some far-off boarding school, she would find a way to come back. Someday, she would find her way home again.

*****

Cole and Lindsay were settled in the sailboat, and Danny was untying the knot that held it to the dock telling them Beau's theory when Lindsay started screaming, "There she is! There she is!"

Cole turned quickly and scanned in the direction of her sister's pointed finger.

"Thank God!" Cole shouted. Cole and Lindsay both leaned into each other and hugged. Lindsay started crying for the second time this summer and what was most likely the second time in her life. Cole quickly followed suit.

Danny was on the dock guiding Tizzy in and grabbing at the rope she threw him. He tied the boat back to the spot it had been in only a few hours before and helped Tizzy step out. She hung her head as her aunts gathered around her, squeezing her, patting her back, and holding her at arm's length, checking her for any injuries.

"Thank God you're home," Cole held Tizzy close and whispered in her ear. Tizzy hadn't yet said a word, and Lindsay and Cole finally stood back, their relief giving way to their frustration and fear. "Why did you go out alone? We were scared out of our minds."

Tizzy picked her head up, and even though she seemed completely exhausted, her eyes were on fire. "I heard you." The tone of Tizzy's voice was a warning to Danny that this was a private family conversation. After making sure the boat was secure, he slipped back onto the beach. "I heard you this morning in the kitchen," Tizzy continued.

Cole and Lindsay both looked at each other and then at Tizzy, questions in their eyes. "Heard what?" Lindsay asked, the confusion seeping out of her.

"That you're sending me away. That you guys are leaving. Going back home. Well, guess what? This is my home!" Tizzy screamed. "This isn't fair!" Tizzy pushed past her aunts and ran back to the beach and on toward the path that led back up the bluff to camp.

Realization dawned in Lindsay's mind seconds after Tizzy ran away. "She heard me say that we had to call Evergreen." Lindsay's heart broke in that moment for what Tizzy must have thought she heard. "We need to go fix this." Cole and Lindsay followed in Tizzy's footsteps, only stopping to let Danny know that everything would be okay and that Cole would call him later to fill him in. The sisters were silent on their way back to the house wondering how to fix the broken heart that belonged to their niece and knowing that the only way was to come completely clean with their plans for the future.

*****

"Tiz? We're going to come in, okay? This is all a misunderstanding." Cole's soft voice broke through Tizzy's bedroom door, and she and Lindsay entered Tizzy's room. Tizzy was lying on her bed, Pip once again at her side, with her head buried in her pillow. The picture of Ann and Jack looked on from the bedside table, smiling encouragement at Cole and Lindsay as they stepped in to try and heal their child's broken heart.

"Tizzy," Lindsay began as she and Cole each sat down on a side of the bed, "I think you misunderstood what we were talking about this morning."

"I didn't. I heard you say you were sending me to a boarding school. Evergreen something." Tizzy's voice was raw with hurt.

"No," Lindsay corrected gently. "You heard us say we had to call the Evergreen Boarding School." Lindsay looked across at Cole and smiled. "At the beginning of summer, after your parent's accident and before Cole or I even came here, we weren't sure what the future held. We contacted Evergreen School as an *option*. We need to call them on Monday to let them know you won't be attending there in the fall." Tizzy shifted and turned her head to look at Lindsay and then Cole.

"I won't?"

"No, honey," Cole continued, "how can you go to school *there* when you live *here*? With us."

Tizzy was afraid it was too good to be true. "But you said you had to get flights back home and that I wouldn't be happy about the news."

"Well, yeah, Tiz, we have to go back to where we used to live to get all our stuff. And I'm pretty sure I said that *some people* wouldn't be happy about it. My boss isn't going to be too happy when I quit." Lindsay giggled and rubbed Tizzy's back. "This is our home, Tizzy."

"We belong here, with you," Cole said and leaned in to hug Tizzy.

"And Ruthie and Pip and Sprint and Summer and Scout and all the other animals." Lindsay laughed out loud now. "I know I've said this before, but living on a summer camp with a barnyard full of animals is not what I imagined for my life." Lindsay leaned down to whisper in Tizzy's ear, "It's even better."

Chapter 21

Lindsay woke Cole early the next morning while it was still dark out. "Cole," Lindsay whispered, "it's time to get up. We've got work to do."

Cole opened her eyes groggily and rolled off the bed. "Fine, fine, I'll be down in a minute. Pour me a cup of coffee. I'm going to need it today."

Lindsay laughed. *There is a first time for everything,* she thought and went downstairs to put away the green tea.

*****

The two sisters braided manes and tails on all the barn horses that they hadn't finished yesterday. They raked the sand in the arena and then went to the deck on the main house to hang the green, blue, and white bunting over the railings. The event started at eleven, so they could expect people to start showing up in a couple of hours. They finished their decorating and went into the house to make breakfast for Tizzy.

"Here, Tiz, orange juice and morning glory muffins. The breakfast of champions." Lindsay set the plate of food down in front of a sleepy-eyed Tizzy. She had slept hard after all the commotion of yesterday.

"Our mom used to always make morning glory muffins for us on the day of trick riding shows. She said it was good luck." Cole winked at her niece who was enjoying the breakfast.

"What's this?" Tizzy pointed to the small white box that was wrapped with a satin bow and placed in the center of the table.

"Well,"—Cole and Lindsay exchanged looks—"we know your birthday isn't until Tuesday, but we thought you might want your gift early so you can wear it today." Tizzy couldn't believe she had almost forgotten it was her thirteenth birthday next week. With so much going on, she hadn't even thought about it.

"Go ahead, open it up." Cole handed the small box to Tizzy.

Unwrapping it gently, Tizzy set aside the top of the box and pulled back the tissue paper. Inside was a round silver locket about the size of a quarter. There was a horseshoe engraved on the front of the locket.

"It was our mother's, your grandmother's, locket." Cole took a sip of her coffee and watched Tizzy tracing the horseshoe with her finger. "Go ahead, open it." Tizzy undid the clasp and opened the locket. Inside on the left was a small picture of her and her parents when she was a baby. On the other side was a picture of her mom and aunts on horseback when they were young girls. "Your whole family is in there, Tizzy. So we'll always be with you."

Tizzy put the necklace on and knew she would never take it off.

Chapter 22

"Welcome, everyone, to the first annual Green Hills Adventure Triathlon!" The community had come out in droves. Lindsay almost couldn't believe how many people had shown up. There must have been close to two hundred people there. Cole continued with the introduction, "We want to thank Camp Still Waters next door for participating and all of you for coming out to support our campers and participants. Here at Green Hills, we believe that every child, girl or boy, deserves a chance at adventure. We hope to expose our campers to new activities and help them gain confidence while having fun. With that in mind, we created this triathlon with the hope of working with our neighboring camps to create a stronger community. This friendly competition consists of three events: sailing, mountain biking, and finally, barrel racing. All of the competitors will participate in and be timed in each event. Their times will be added up at the end of the competition, and the camper with the lowest completion time wins." Cole paused and glanced over at Lindsay, Tizzy, and Ruthie. "My sisters and I grew up on this camp. We watched our parents build this place from the ground up. This camp is our legacy, a legacy that we are proud of and hope to continue. This event started as a way for us to bring awareness to what we do here, encourage and empower girls to be confident in their ability to try new and adventurous things. Thankfully, this event has turned into much more. It has allowed us to con-nect with the camp next door, Still Waters, and to connect with all of you, our community. We want to thank you for coming, and hope you'll stick around for the BBQ after the competition."

Cole looked around at all the people surround-ing the riding arena. She saw a lot of familiar faces from the island, some reaching as far back as her childhood and saw many more that she didn't rec-ognize. She hoped all their hard work fixing up the camp would pay off. Wishing for a little luck on their side she crossed her fingers. "We'll start by heading down to the beach at Still Waters and end back up here. Let the games begin!" Lindsay and Cole latched arms and led the way to the trail that would take all the spectators down to the beach. The visitors were talking amongst themselves, pointing at the cabins as they passed by on their way to the lawn. Cole looked at the cabins and was glad they had repainted the doors and hung the camp flags out front. They looked fresh and inviting. Passing the main house, she noticed how bright and cheery it looked with the bunting hanging from the deck. "We should keep that up all year," she whispered to Lindsay.

"Hmmm? Oh yeah, sorry, I'm listening to the people behind us," she whispered back. "We're getting great reviews." Lindsay smiled and winked at her sister. She had a feeling this was going to turn out even better than she had hoped.

*****

The sailing and mountain biking portions of the triathlon went off without a hitch. All the competitors did really well and were having a lot of fun, not taking it too seriously. The crowd cheered loudly for each camper, locals rooting for the underdogs and parents in awe as they watched their kids compete in a completely new sport. A lot of the Still Waters' parents seemed impressed that their boys were so competitive at the mountain biking, and many of the girl's parents loved the idea that their daughters were able to learn to sail as well. There was a lot of buzz amongst the audience about the benefits of the camps working together. When everyone finally made it back up to the arena for the last event, barrel racing, they quickly took their seats in the bleachers that had been set up around the arena. Ruthie had helped to tack up a couple of the camp horses, and the kids were going to take turns.

Cole and Lindsay stood in the arena, keeping a close eye on the beginning riders, but everything went smoothly. The new riders took the barrels at a jog while Tizzy and a few others went faster at a lope. Tizzy was the last to run and had the crowd on their feet as Sprint whirled around the last barrel and raced home. Everyone there knew that the spunky girl with the long auburn braid had won. She had excelled in every aspect of the triathlon, and it was fun to see a young girl compete with such confidence.

After hugging and kissing Tizzy when she dismounted, Cole and Lindsay snuck off toward the barn. Danny now stood in the center of the arena while Tizzy, Beau, and Ruthie rolled the barrels out of the way. "Excuse me, everyone!" He shouted to regain the audience's attention. "We hope you have all had fun watching our campers today. At Green Hills Adventure Camp and at Still Waters, we strive to push our campers to try new things and to build confidence in the process. We hope what you've seen today has helped you to get a feeling for what we do here all summer. We will be totaling the timed scores of all the competitors and posting them on a board at the BBQ, but I want to remind everyone that this event wasn't about the fastest time or winners or losers but about trying something out of your comfort zone, and at that, you've all succeeded." The crowd clapped, and few of the dads whistled. "Before you head over to the lawn for the BBQ, we have one more special event. As most of you know, Green Hills specializes in adventure sports. Mountain biking, kayaking, and barrel racing have been the focus here for decades. Starting next year, however, they are going to be adding a new event, one that the camp operators are going to showcase for you now. Please put your hands together for two trick-riding sisters hailing from Orcas Island and finally back home for good, Cole and Lindsay Burns!"

Danny swept his arm to the side as Lindsay and Cole galloped in on the backs of Summer and Scout. Tizzy had pressed play on the sound system, and an old country Western song began to thrum through the arena. Tizzy led the cheering as people clapped and laughed at the two sisters who were obviously having the time of their lives.

Ruthie couldn't believe her eyes. It was like a flashback to twenty years ago. Cole and Lindsay had changed into jeans and matching denim shirts with red stitching, wore white cowboy hats, and had braided Scout and Summer's hair so that you could hardly tell the two horses apart. *They look just like they used to when they competed,* Ruthie thought, and a huge smiled blossomed on her face.

Cole and Tizzy galloped around the oval arena several times, waving at the crowd before they began the short routine they had been practicing for weeks now. They swung their legs off on one side, bouncing them quickly on the ground before leaping back into the saddle and then quickly went up onto the horse's backs in a standing position. The two sisters waved to the crowd, who were stunned into silence before bursting into applause. They ended the show with a trick called Roman riding. Cole pulled Summer up beside Lindsay and Scout, and then each sister stepped one foot onto the other horse's back. They rode once around the arena, Lindsay standing in front of Cole, each with one foot balanced on Summer and the other on Scout. The music finally came to an end, and the sisters gracefully hopped back onto their own horse and pulled up to stop in the middle of the ring. They took off their hats and waved them in the air, the applause continuing for a long time. Tizzy couldn't believe what she had just seen. She had only ever seen trick riders that good at the Ellensburg Rodeo when her parents had taken her one year. She had no idea her aunts could do that.

"Please, everyone, make your way to the lawn for the BBQ and entertainment we have set up there. Thank you again for coming. We hope you have a minute to check out the camp booths where we can answer any questions you may have and help you sign your children up for camp next year." Danny stood in front of the bleachers and began to help usher guests toward the lawn. Tizzy ran out into the arena to her aunts.

"That was"—Tizzy's eyes were wide, and her mount hung open—"that was awesome." She leapt into Lindsay's arms and squeezed her tight before doing the same to Cole. "I had no idea you guys could do that. You're incredible." Cole and Lindsay just laughed and hugged Tizzy back.

"That was just our rusty performance. Wait until we get back into it." Cole patted Summer's shoulder. "These two sure know what they're doing." Cole indicated Scout and Summer and pulled treats out of her jean pocket for them.

"Ann kept them in incredible shape. I can't wait to see where we can take them," Lindsay added.

"Are we really adding trick riding sessions to the camp next year?" Tizzy couldn't believe it.

"Of course, that's what we know best." Cole winked at Tizzy and handed her the reigns. "You did awesome in the triathlon, Tizzy. We're so proud of you."

"It was fun learning something new with the sailing. I guess I had forgotten how much I like to compete too. I'm thinking I may sign up for the barrel racing competition next month at the San Juan County rodeo. I'm going to have to put in a lot of practice, but I think I'm ready."

"Of course you are," Lindsay said, "you're the best around." She smiled at Tizzy who was fingering her locket. "Hey, Tiz, we have to run over to manage the camp booth at the BBQ. Can you just untack Summer and Scout and then head on over? I'm sure you're going to want to check out the standings of the triathlon, and that will give me a second to get them up."

"Sure, it'll just take a minute, then I'll be right over." Tizzy grabbed the reins from her aunts and led the horses back toward the barn.

Cole and Lindsay walked out the arena gate, and when they were sure Tizzy was out of earshot, Lindsay whispered, "Come on, we've only got a few minutes to get everyone ready," and the two sisters took off running.

*****

"Hey, everybody, we have a big favor to ask of you," Lindsay called out to all the guests milling around the lawn drinking the lemonade and mint tea Ruthie had set out. "Our niece, Tizzy, whom many of you know, is turning thirteen this next week, and we thought this would be the perfect time to give her a little surprise party." Cole and Lindsay grabbed baskets they had hid under a nearby table and started handing out sparklers to all the guests. "She'll be here in just a moment. If everyone could grab a sparkler and shout surprise when she rounds the corner from the barn, this would make an amazing birthday party for her. She deserves it." Friends from town came up to Cole and grabbed some of the sparklers and started passing them around. Ruthie walked over carrying a two-tier birthday cake with a small replica of Sprint on top.

Danny, who had just finished hanging a banner that said "Happy Birthday, Tizzy", between two tall pine trees, was at the corner of the house peeking toward the barn where Tizzy wouldn't be able to see him.

"Quick, light the candles and sparklers," Danny called. "She just left the barn." Ruthie, Cole, and Lindsay all lit their sparklers, and groups of people held their sparklers to the flame until everyone's was lit. "Ssshhh!" Danny ran back to the crowd and stood next to Cole.

Tizzy rounded the far corner of the house and looked toward the lawn, expecting to see the BBQ in full swing. "Surprise!" everyone chorused.

There, in the front yard crowded with campers' families and neighbors, stood her friends and family lit up like fireworks. Tears sprung up in Tizzy's eyes as she realized that even with her parents gone, she had a family with Cole, Lindsay and Ruthie. They stood front and center smiling back at her, Lindsay holding out a sparkler for her and Cole a bouquet of yellow balloons. They were quite a sight, her aunts in matching outfits and cowboy hats, something she hadn't ever expected to see. Tizzy began to laugh right there on the corner of the lawn, tears streaming down her face and her cheeks hurting from the biggest smile she had worn all summer.

"How long have you guys been planning this?" Tizzy asked her aunts.

"For weeks," Cole answered, and Tizzy realized that her aunts must have made up their minds that they were staying long ago. "We know your parents always planned a special birthday party for you every year. We want you to know that you still have lot of people in this world who love you." Tizzy looked around at all the glowing sparklers and knew in her heart that it was true. She turned to Ruthie who was holding the cake and took a second before closing her eyes and blowing out her candles. She smiled when she realized she didn't even have anything to wish for.

Chapter 23

Decorative lights that Cole and Lindsay had strung between the trees on the lawn lit up the night sky as the eating, laughing, and dancing continued into the night. The BBQ turned birthday party was a huge success, Lindsay realized as she looked down at the long list of campers who had already signed up for next year. Parents had put down deposit payments that would help tide the camp over through the winter.

Tizzy stood in the center of all the activity, saying hello to guests and chatting with Danielle, who had shown up with her parents at the end of the trick-riding show. "Did you see who your newest camper will be next year?" Danielle asked Tizzy.

"No way!" Tizzy couldn't believe it. "You're coming here?"

"Yes!" Danielle shrieked, and guests nearby turned to look at the two girls who were laughing and hugging wildly. "My parents went over to look at the booth your aunts set up, and they met Lindsay. Of course, they had talked to her on the phone earlier this summer, but meeting her sealed the deal. Once she mentioned she was bringing in a marketing strategy she had designed for her firm in New York to boost the camp's business, my parents signed me up. They think Green Hills is going to be 'the next big thing.'" Danielle did air quotes to emphasize her parent's words. "They always want to be in on the next big thing. I don't care about the reasons as long as I get to come here instead of going back to ERA. Besides, your aunts were awesome on those horses! I have to learn to do that next year. I wouldn't let my parents send me anywhere else," Danielle stated emphatically.

"I can't believe it." Tizzy just laughed.

"Well, believe it. I'm staying the whole summer."

*****

Lindsay and Ruthie kept making the rounds, introducing themselves to new faces and answering questions about the camp. Tizzy had just spotted Cole and Danny dancing and laughing with each other and was watching them when she felt a hand on her shoulder.

"Hey, Tizzy."

"Oh, hey, Beau." She hadn't seen Beau since the competition and was afraid he had left without saying good-bye.

"You did awesome in the triathlon. First place. I'm going to have to practice barrel racing more so that next year you have some real competition," he teased.

Tizzy smiled. She had won the competition and by a lot. "Thanks. It was a lot of fun."

"Maybe we can trade sailing lessons for riding lessons?"

"Sure, I'd love that." Tizzy realized that she was already looking forward to next summer and hanging out with Beau. "So you're coming back for sure next summer?"

"Of course. But I'll be back before then." Beau's smile deepened. "Danny is going to be teaching more mountain biking clinics. One weekend a month. My parents already signed me up, so I'll be back in a few weeks.

"That's great. I guess I'll see you then." Tizzy blushed when she realized this was her best birthday ever.

*****

"Thank you so much for coming!" Cole called out as the last car left their property and headed back toward town. Tizzy, Cole, and Lindsay had stood near the camp entrance, saying good-bye to all their guests

161

and letting many of them know that they would see them next summer.

"We did it." Lindsay blew out a huge sigh of relief. "I can't believe we did it."

"Of course we did," Cole answered, "and we have one more thing to show you, Tizzy." Lindsay and Cole smiled at each other and took Tizzy's arms. "This way," Cole said as they led her out into the road.

"What else could there possibly be?"

"Close your eyes and turn around," Lindsay ordered. Tizzy closed her eyes and turned so that she was facing the camp's entrance. "Okay, open them," Lindsay squealed.

Tizzy opened her eyes and, in the fading light, could just make out the brand-new camp sign that stood out on the post over the drive. "Welcome to Green Hills", and under that, "where adventure begins."

"It's perfect," Tizzy whispered. She looked at Cole and then at Lindsay. "I didn't think life could ever be perfect again, and now it is."

*****

The three girls were still standing at the gate when a large black Mercedes SUV pulled up and honked its horn. The back door opened and Danielle hopped out carrying a box with her. "Tizzy, I almost forgot," she squealed. Lindsay and Cole looked on as Danielle handed Tizzy a long box with a bow on top.

"Your birthday present. I had my parents bring them from Boston. Your aunts told me your size." Tizzy took the lid off the box and saw the most exquisite pair of black leather lace-up English riding boots. She gasped and touched them gently.

"They're for show jumping. Next summer, I get to be *your* coach," Danielle said and threw her arms around Tizzy in a hug. Before Tizzy could even say thank you, Danielle had run back to the car and hopped in. Tizzy laughed to herself, she could hardly wait.

About the Author

Laura Weigel Douglas grew up reading thousands and thousands of books....mostly about horses. After reading her way through her first series, The Saddle Club, in elementary school, Laura knew two things: someday she wanted to write a book of her own, and she wanted a horse. This book is checking the first wish off that list.

Laura enjoys traveling with her family, visiting the local library and spending time with her sisters. Her love of reading, adventure and the outdoors combined to create this novel, When the Stars Lead Home. Laura lives in the Pacific Northwest with her husband, daughter, two dogs and a cat in a house that sometimes feels like Green Hills Adventure Camp. She couldn't be more grateful.

CPSIA information can be obtained
at www.ICGtesting.com
Printed in the USA
LVOW03s0303190417
531320LV00001B/6/P